THE SCARLET
and Other Stories

JACK LONDON

THE SCARLET PLAGUE
and Other Stories

ALAN SUTTON PUBLISHING LIMITED

'The Scarlet Plague' first published in 1915
'The Dream of Debs' first published in 1914
'The Shadow and the Flash' first published in 1906
'The Unparalleled Invasion' first published in 1914
'The Heathen' first published in 1911
'The Mexican' first published in 1913

First published in this edition in the United Kingdom in 1995
Alan Sutton Publishing Limited
Phoenix Mill · Far Thrupp · Stroud · Gloucestershire

First published in this edition in the United States of America in 1995
Alan Sutton Publishing Inc
83 Washington Street · Dover · NH 03820

British Library Cataloguing-in-Publication Data

A catalogue record for this book is available from the British Library.

ISBN 0–7509–0879–3

Library of Congress Cataloging-in-Publication Data applied for

Cover picture: *detail from* Armageddon, *1852 (Revelations 16:16) by Joseph Paul Pettit (1812–82).*
(Photograph courtesy of York City Art Gallery/Bridgeman Art Library, London)

Typeset in 10/11 Bembo.
Typsetting and origination by
Alan Sutton Publishing Limited.
Printed in Great Britain by
The Guernsey Press Company Limited,
Guernsey, Channel Islands.

CONTENTS

BIOGRAPHICAL NOTE

JACK LONDON (1876–1916) was born in San Francisco on 12 January 1876. His mother, Flora Wellman, was a music teacher and spiritualist; his father, John Chaney, an astrologer. They were not married and John Chaney refused to acknowledge his son. Shortly after Jack's birth, however, Flora married a John London who brought with him his two daughters into the household. Life was hard for the London family, struggling to make ends meet, and Jack's mother was too busy to give him the attention which he craved, but she was able to send him to school for some years. There the world of literature made its first impact on him. The romantic world of Ouida's *Signa* stirred his earliest dreams of making good, travelling and achieving success. He had to leave school when he was fifteen, and he went to work in a cannery. It was soul-destroying work, and the romantic Jack soon escaped to become an oyster pirate. Later, he changed allegiances by joining the rough-handed fishing control who tackled the pirates on the high seas.

He was a popular boy and showed every sign of becoming a delinquent group leader, but when he was seventeen he broke away from the gang in search of adventure, joining a sealing expedition into the North West Pacific. His experiences during those five months led to the publication of his first prose work, *Typhoon off the Coast of Japan* (1893), a prize-winning essay. This success encouraged Jack in his endeavours to make progress through hard work, but his willingness to do manual work in an electrical company was exploited and, disheartened and exhausted, he felt that he had no alternative but to join Kelly's Army. It was his adventures with this band of protesting unemployed men and, later, on his own as a vagabond on the road, eventually ending up in Eyrie County Penitentiary, that were instrumental in forming Jack's personal socialist philosophy. They provided the material for his novel *The Road* (1907), the precursor of the American tramp literature, such as that of Jack Kerouac.

Horrified by his experiences at Eyrie, mixing with vagrants of the lowest social order, Jack returned home, determined this time to improve his chances by studying. His mother supported him as he succeeded in passing exams to university. Jack, however, had seen too much of life, and was no longer prepared to spend four years in 'passionless studies'. He left

Berkeley after only one term, now resolved to make his own way as a writer, once again maintaining himself by manual work. But those early literary experiments were immature and unsuccessful, and for a second time he fled from a grim situation, this time by joining the Klondyke Gold Rush in 1897. This expedition did not make Jack rich, although it did give him time to study further and to mature intellectually. He read Darwin, Huxley, Herbert Spenser, Kipling, Milton and Dante. He developed his own direct and concise style of writing and learnt to describe mental suffering metaphorically, through physical torment. When he returned to California, he settled to writing full-time, and after little more than a year of financial misery the *Atlantic Monthly* accepted *An Odyssey of the North* (1899). Then the publishers Houghton Mifflin offered to publish his Alaskan stories, *The Son of the Wolf* (1900). At the age of twenty-four Jack was establishing himself in his chosen profession. From now on, until his death, he was to publish regularly, with never less than one novel a year to his name. A self-made man, he encouraged the myth that developed around him. Like the wolf, which he adopted as his symbol, he was both a loner and a leader; with a charismatic personality he worked to develop an image of himself as slightly larger than life.

His search for domestic security led to his marriage to Bessie Maddern and two daughters. The couple had little in common, and Jack soon resumed his platonic relationship with the socialist, Anna Strunsky, collaborating with her in writing, under pseudonyms, a series of philosophical letters about the nature of love. In spite of the love which she knew Jack felt for her, Anna broke off the relationship when he left for a visit to Europe in 1902. He stayed for some weeks in London, visiting the worst areas of the East End as a down-and-out, obtaining material for *The People of the Abyss* (1903), a sociological study of London slums.

When Jack returned to California, he attempted to patch up his marriage and resumed his leadership of the Crowd, a group of literary and artistic Californians. He produced *The Call of the Wild*, his first masterpiece, in 1903, to be followed by the equally successful *Sea Wolf* (1904). But his personal life was not so successful. He had now fallen madly in love with Charmian Kittredge, a woman five years older than himself, whom he eventually married after spending six months abroad as a war correspondent in the Russian-Japanese War and divorcing Bessie in 1904. He bought a ranch in Glen Ellen, where he lived with Charmian and began to realize his dream of creating a productive farm. He had always attached great importance to physical health and a good physique, so it was with difficulty that at this time he first had to accept that his body was ageing. His desire to preserve good health was soon to become an obsession with him. In the meantime his attempt to settle down to domesticity was portrayed in *White Fang* (1907), the story of 'the evolution, the civilization of a dog'.

Jack London had long been a member of the Socialist Labour Party, as well as a political lecturer and essayist. He wrote several novels predicting the evolution of socialism, including *The Iron Heel* (1908). The latter was a grim study of fascism, and precursor of the works of Huxley and Orwell. At the same time, he was still developing his own personal myth, as a literary cult figure, and his most extravagant gesture was probably the construction of the sailing boat, *The Snark*, on which he proposed to travel the seven seas for seven years, free from worry. The building of the boat almost bankrupted him, interrupted as it was by the earthquake and fire of 1906, which also caused damage to his ranch. The journey itself was little less than disastrous, terminating after only two years, during which time Jack had not escaped the financial problems of the ranch but had suffered from a variety of fevers and infections. His disillusionment is revealed in *Martin Eden* (1909), a semi-autobiographical novel which concludes with the suicide of the central character.

The end of the adventure for Jack was hospitalization and convalescence in Australia. He was treated with arsenic for yaws, a skin complaint, and this treatment was to scar his body and damage his internal organs permanently.

After he returned to California in 1909, he turned his attention to the development and enlargement of Beauty Ranch. He wrote primarily to make money, and he was successful in his aim. For a while all went well, but at the end of 1910 Charmian gave birth to a baby who died two days later, and then in the following year Jack's ailing body troubled him both physically and mentally. He treated himself with Salvarsan, an arsenic compound which did little to help him; and drank excessively to kill his pain. In spite of his suffering, he remained extrovert, welcoming guests of all classes to his ranch and employing ex-convicts from San Quentin jail. He followed a strict timetable, writing every morning. One of the important books completed during this time was *John Barleycorn* (1913), another semi-autobiographical novel showing the dangers of indulging in alcohol. By 1914 Jack was taking mixtures of belladonna, morphia, heroin and strychnine, and it was at this time that he wrote *The Star Rover*, an ambitious novel which attempts to attain the mythical in its thematic development, and uses a prison background which had been described to London by Ed Morrell, one of the ex-convicts he had befriended.

Fighting disease and pain, Jack hid his illnesses from the public eye and, in 1914, took a job as correspondent covering the Mexican Revolution. He made two holiday trips to Hawaii in 1915–16, but his indulgence in raw meat and alcohol, as well as all the medical drugs with which he was injecting himself, were wearing out his system, and on 22 November 1916 he died at Beauty Ranch after injecting himself, apparently accidentally, with a fatal overdose of drugs.

His books, with the exception of *White Fang* and *Call of the Wild* (important originals of the sociobiological genre), are largely neglected in Great Britain, but they have enjoyed regular popularity in America and France, and Jack London is one of the most widely read Western writers in Russia.

SHEILA MICHELL

THE SCARLET PLAGUE

CHAPTER ONE

The way led along upon what had once been the embankment of a railroad. But no train had run upon it for many years. The forest on either side swelled up the slopes of the embankment and crested across it in a green wave of trees and bushes. The trail was as narrow as a man's body, and was no more than a wild-animal runway. Occasionally, a piece of rusty iron, showing through the forest-mould, advertised that the rail and the ties still remained. In one place, a ten-inch tree, bursting through at a connection, had lifted the end of a rail clearly into view. The tie had evidently followed the rail, held to it by the spike long enough for its bed to be filled with gravel and rotten leaves, so that now the crumbling, rotten timber thrust itself up at a curious slant. Old as the road was, it was manifest that it had been of the mono-rail type.

An old man and a boy travelled along this runway. They moved slowly, for the old man was very old, a touch of palsy made his movements tremulous, and he leaned heavily upon his staff. A rude skull-cap of goat-skin protected his head from the sun. From beneath this fell a scant fringe of stained and dirty-white hair. A visor, ingeniously made from a large leaf, shielded his eyes, and from under this he peered at the way of his feet on the trail. His beard, which should have been snow-white but which showed the same weather-wear and camp-stain as his hair, fell nearly to his waist in a great tangled mass. About his chest and shoulders hung a single, mangy garment of goat-skin. His arms and legs, withered and skinny, betokened extreme age, as well as did their sunburn and scars and scratches betoken long years of exposure to the elements.

The boy, who led the way, checking the eagerness of his muscles to the slow progress of the elder, likewise wore a single garment − a ragged-edged piece of bear-skin, with a hole in the middle through which he had thrust his head. He could not have been more than twelve years old. Tucked coquettishly over one ear was the freshly severed tail of a pig. In one hand he carried a medium-sized bow and an arrow. On his back was a quiverful of arrows. From a sheath hanging about his neck on a thong, projected the battered handle of a hunting-knife. He was as brown as a berry, and walked softly, with almost a catlike tread. In marked contrast

1

with his sun-burned skin were his eyes – blue, deep blue, but keen and sharp as a pair of gimlets. They seemed to bore into all about him in a way that was habitual. As he went along he smelled things as well, his distended, quivering nostrils carrying to his brain an endless series of messages from the outside world. Also, his hearing was acute, and had been so trained that it operated automatically. Without conscious effort, he heard all the slight sounds in the apparent quiet – heard, and differentiated, and classified these sounds – whether they were of the wind rustling the leaves, of the humming of bees and gnats, of the distant rumble of the sea that drifted to him only in lulls, or of the gopher, just under his foot, shoving a pouchful of earth into the entrance of his hole.

Suddenly he became alertly tense. Sound, sight, and odour had given him a simultaneous warning. His hand went back to the old man, touching him, and the pair stood still. Ahead, at one side of the top of the embankment, arose a crackling sound, and the boy's gaze was fixed on the tops of the agitated bushes. Then a large bear, a grizzly, crashed into view, and likewise stopped abruptly, at sight of the humans. He did not like them, and growled querulously. Slowly the boy fitted the arrow to the bow, and slowly he pulled the bowstring taut. But he never removed his eyes from the bear. The old man peered from under his green leaf at the danger, and stood as quietly as the boy. For a few seconds this mutual scrutinizing went on; then, the bear betraying a growing irritability, the boy, with a movement of his head, indicated that the old man must step aside from the trail and go down the embankment. The boy followed, going backward, still holding the bow taut and ready. They waited till a crashing among the bushes from the opposite side of the embankment told them the bear had gone on. The boy grinned as he led back to the trail.

'A big un, Granser,' he chuckled.

The old man shook his head.

'They get thicker every day,' he complained in a thin, undependable falsetto. 'Who'd have thought I'd live to see the time when a man would be afraid of his life on the way to the Cliff House. When I was a boy, Edwin, men and women and little babies used to come out here from San Francisco by tens of thousands on a nice day. And there weren't any bears then. No, sir. They used to pay money to look at them in cages, they were that rare.'

'What is money, Granser?'

Before the old man could answer, the boy recollected and triumphantly shoved his hand into a pouch under his bear-skin and pulled forth a battered and tarnished silver dollar. The old man's eyes glistened, as he held the coin close to them.

'I can't see,' he muttered. 'You look and see if you can make out the date, Edwin.'

The boy laughed.

'You're a great Granser,' he cried delightedly, 'always making believe them little marks mean something.'

The old man manifested an accustomed chagrin as he brought the coin back again close to his own eyes.

'2012,' he shrilled, and then fell to cackling grotesquely. 'That was the year Morgan the Fifth was appointed President of the United States by the Board of Magnates. It must have been one of the last coins minted, for the Scarlet Death came in 2013. Lord! Lord! – think of it! Sixty years ago, and I am the only person alive today, that lived in those times. Where did you find it, Edwin?'

The boy, who had been regarding him with the tolerant curiousness one accords to the prattlings of the feeble-minded, answered promptly:

'I got it off of Hoo-Hoo. He found it when we was herdin' goats down near San Jose last spring. Hoo-Hoo said it was *money*. Ain't you hungry, Granser?'

The ancient caught his staff in a tighter grip and urged along the trail, his old eyes shining greedily.

'I hope Hare-Lip's found a crab . . . or two,' he mumbled. 'They're good eating, crabs, mighty good eating when you've no more teeth and you've got grandsons that love their old grandsire and make a point of catching crabs for him. When I was a boy——'

But Edwin, suddenly stopped by what he saw, was drawing the bowstring on a fitted arrow. He had paused on the brink of a crevasse in the embankment. An ancient culvert had here washed out, and the stream, no longer confined, had cut a passage through the fill. On the opposite side, the end of a rail projected and overhung. It showed rustily through the creeping vines which over-ran it. Beyond, crouching by a bush, a rabbit looked across at him in trembling hesitancy. Fully fifty feet was the distance, but the arrow flashed true; and the transfixed rabbit, crying out in sudden fright and hurt, struggled painfully away into the brush. The boy himself was a flash of brown skin and flying fur as he bounded down the steep wall of the gap and up the other side. His lean muscles were springs of steel that released into graceful and efficient action. A hundred feet beyond, in a tangle of bushes, he overtook the wounded creature, knocked its head on a convenient tree-trunk, and turned it over to Granser to carry.

'Rabbit is good, very good,' the ancient quavered, 'but when it comes to a toothsome delicacy I prefer crab. When I was a boy——'

'Why do you say so much that ain't got no sense?' Edwin impatiently interrupted the other's threatened garrulousness.

The boy did not exactly utter these words, but something that remotely resembled them and that was more guttural and explosive and

economical of qualifying phrases. His speech showed distant kinship with
that of the old man, and the latter's speech was approximately an English
that had gone through a bath of corrupt usage.

'What I want to know,' Edwin continued, 'is why you call crab
"toothsome delicacy?" Crab is crab, ain't it? No one I never heard calls it
such funny things.'

The old man sighed but did not answer, and they moved on in silence.
The surf grew suddenly louder, as they emerged from the forest upon a
stretch of sand dunes bordering the sea. A few goats were browsing
among the sandy hillocks, and a skinclad boy, aided by a wolfish-looking
dog that was only faintly reminiscent of a collie, was watching them.
Mingled with the roar of the surf was a continuous, deep-throated
barking or bellowing, which came from a cluster of jagged rocks a
hundred yards out from shore. Here huge sea-lions hauled themselves up
to lie in the sun or battle with one another. In the immediate foreground
arose the smoke of a fire, tended by a third savage-looking boy. Crouched
near him were several wolfish dogs similar to the one that guarded the
goats.

The old man accelerated his pace, sniffing eagerly as he neared the fire.

'Mussels!' he muttered ecstatically. 'Mussels! and ain't that a crab, Hoo-
Hoo? Ain't that a crab? My, my, you boys are good to your old grandsire.'

Hoo-Hoo, who was apparently of the same age as Edwin, grinned.

'All you want, Granser. I got four.'

The old man's palsied eagerness was pitiful. Sitting down in the sand as
quickly as his stiff limbs would let him, he poked a large rock-mussel
from out of the coals. The heat had forced its shells apart, and the meat,
salmon-coloured, was thoroughly cooked. Between thumb and
forefinger, in trembling haste, he caught the mussel and carried it to his
mouth. But it was too hot, and the next moment as violently ejected.
The old man spluttered with the pain, and tears ran out of his eyes and
down his cheeks.

The boys were true savages, possessing only the cruel humour of the
savage. To them the incident was excruciatingly funny, and they burst
into loud laughter. Hoo-Hoo danced up and down, while Edwin rolled
gleefully on the ground. The boy with the goats came running to join in
the fun.

'Set 'em to cool, Edwin, set 'em to cool,' the old man besought, in the
midst of his grief, making no attempt to wipe away the tears that still
flowed from his eyes. 'And cool a crab, Edwin, too. You know your
grandsire likes crabs.'

From the coals arose a great sizzling, which proceeded from the many
mussels bursting open their shells and exuding their moisture. They were
large shellfish, running from three to six inches in length. The boys raked

them out with sticks and placed them on a large piece of driftwood to cool.

'When I was a boy, we did not laugh at our elders; we respected them.'

The boys took no notice, and Granser continued to babble an incoherent flow of complaint and censure. But this time he was more careful, and did not burn his mouth. All began to eat, using nothing but their hands and making loud mouth-noises and lip-smackings. The third boy, who was called Hare-Lip, slyly deposited a pinch of sand on a mussel the ancient was carrying into his mouth; and when the grit of it bit into the old fellow's mucous membrane and gums, the laughter was again uproarious. He was unaware that a joke had been played on him, and spluttered and spat until Edwin, relenting, gave him a gourd of fresh water with which to wash out his mouth.

'Where's them crabs, Hoo-Hoo?' Edwin demanded. 'Granser's set upon having a snack.'

Again Granser's eyes burned with greediness as a large crab was handed to him. It was a shell with legs and all complete, but the meat had long since departed. With shaky fingers and babblings of anticipation, the old man broke off a leg and found it filled with emptiness.

'The crabs, Hoo-Hoo?' He wailed. 'The crabs?'

'I was foolin', Granser. They ain't no crabs. I never found one.'

The boys were overwhelmed with delight at sight of the tears of senile disappointment, that dribbled down the old man's cheeks. Then, unnoticed, Hoo-Hoo replaced the empty shell with a fresh-cooked crab. Already dismembered, from the cracked legs the white meat sent forth a small cloud of savoury steam. This attracted the old man's nostrils, and he looked down in amazement. The change of his mood to one of joy was immediate. He snuffled and muttered and mumbled, making almost a croon of delight, as he began to eat. Of this the boys took little notice, for it was an accustomed spectacle. Nor did they notice his occasional exclamations and utterances of phrases which meant nothing to them, as, for instance, when he smacked his lips and champed his gums while muttering: 'Mayonnaise! Just think – mayonnaise! And it's sixty years since the last was ever made! Two generations and never a smell of it! Why, in those days it was served in every restaurant with crab.'

When he could eat no more, the old man sighed, wiped his hands on his naked legs, and gazed out over the sea. With the content of a full stomach, he waxed reminiscent.

'To think of it! I've seen this beach alive with men, women, and children on a pleasant Sunday. And there weren't any bears to eat them up, either. And right up there on the cliff was a big restaurant where you could get anything you wanted to eat. Four million people lived in San Francisco then. And now, in the whole city and country there aren't forty all told. And out there on the sea were ships and ships always to be seen, going in for the Golden Gate or coming out. And airships in the air – dirigibles and flying machines. They could travel two hundred miles an hour. The mail contracts with the New York and San Francisco Limited demanded that for the minimum. There was a chap, a Frenchman, I forget his name, who succeeded in making three hundred; but the thing was risky, too risky for conservative persons. But he was on the right clue, and he would have managed it if it hadn't been for the Great Plague. When I was a boy, there were men alive who remembered the coming of the first aeroplanes, and now I have lived to see the last of them, and that sixty years ago.'

The old man babbled on, unheeded by the boys, who were long accustomed to his garrulousness, and whose vocabularies, besides, lacked the greater portion of the words he used. It was noticeable that in these rambling soliloquies his English seemed to recrudesce into better construction and phraseology. But when he talked directly with the boys it lapsed, largely, into their own uncouth and simpler forms.

'But there weren't many crabs in those days,' the old man wandered on. 'They were fished out, and they were great delicacies. The open season was only a month long, too. And now crabs are accessible the whole year round. Think of it – catching all the crabs you want, any time you want, in the surf of the Cliff House beach!'

A sudden commotion among the goats brought the boys to their feet. The dogs about the fire rushed to join their snarling fellow who guarded the goats, while the goats themselves stampeded in the direction of their human protectors. A half-dozen forms, lean and grey, glided about on the sand hillocks or faced the bristling dogs. Edwin arched an arrow that fell short. But Hare-Lip, with a sling such as David carried into battle against Goliath, hurled a stone through the air that whistled from the speed of its flight. It fell squarely among the wolves and caused them to slink away towards the dark depths of the eucalyptus forest.

The boys laughed and lay down again in the sand, while Granser sighed ponderously. He had eaten too much, and with hands clasped on his paunch, the fingers interlaced, he resumed his maunderings.

'"The fleeting systems lapse like foam",' he mumbled what was evidently a quotation. 'That's it – foam, and fleeting. All man's toil upon the planet was just so much foam. He domesticated the serviceable animals, destroyed the hostile ones, and cleared the land of its wild vegetation. And then he passed, and the flood of primordial life rolled back again, sweeping his handiwork away – the weeds and the forest inundated his fields, the beasts of prey swept over his flocks, and now there are wolves on the Cliff House beach.' He was appalled by the thought. 'Where four million people disported themselves, the wild wolves roam today, and the savage progeny of our loins, with prehistoric weapons, defend themselves against the fanged despoilers. Think of it! And all because of the Scarlet Death——'

The adjective had caught Hare-Lip's ear.

'He's always saying that,' he said to Edwin. 'What is *scarlet*?'

'"The scarlet of the maples can shake me like the cry of bugles going by",' the old man quoted.

'It's red,' Edwin answered the question. 'And you don't know it because you come from the Chauffeur Tribe. They never did know nothing, none of them. *Scarlet* is red – I know that.'

'Red is red, ain't it?' Hare-Lip grumbled. 'Then what's the good of gettin' cocky and calling it scarlet?'

'Granser, what for do you always say so much what nobody knows?' he asked. 'Scarlet ain't anything, but red is red. Why don't you say red, then?'

'Red is not the right word,' was the reply. 'The plague was scarlet. The whole face and body turned scarlet in an hour's time. Don't I know? Didn't I see enough of it? And I am telling you it was scarlet because – well, because it *was* scarlet. There is no other word for it.'

'Red is good enough for me,' Hare-Lip muttered obstinately. 'My dad calls red red, and he ought to know. He says everybody died of the Red Death.'

'Your dad is a common fellow, descended from a common fellow,' Granser retorted heatedly. 'Don't I know the beginning of the Chauffeurs? Your grandsire was a chauffeur, servant, and without education. He worked for other persons. But your grandmother was of good stock, only the children did not take after her. Don't I remember when I first met them, catching fish at Lake Temescal?'

'What is *education*?' Edwin asked.

'Calling red scarlet,' Hare-Lip sneered, then returned to the attack on Granser. 'My dad told me, an' he got it from his dad afore he croaked, that your wife was a Santa Rosan an' that she was sure no account. He said she was a *hash-slinger* before the Red Death, though I don't know what a *hash-slinger* is. You can tell me, Edwin.'

But Edwin shook his head in token of ignorance.

'It is true, she was a waitress,' Granser acknowledged. 'But she was a good woman, and your mother was her daughter. Women were very scarce in the days after the Plague. She was the only wife I could find, even if she was a *hash-slinger*, as your father calls it. But it is not nice to talk about our progenitors that way.'

'Dad says that the wife of the first Chauffeur was a *lady*——'

'What's a *lady*?' Hoo-Hoo demanded.

'A *lady's* a Chauffeur squaw,' was the quick reply of Hare-Lip.

'The first Chauffeur was Bill, a common fellow, as I said before,' the old man expounded; 'but his wife was a lady, a great lady. Before the Scarlet Death she was the wife of Van Warden. He was President of the Board of Industrial Magnates, and was one of the dozen men who ruled America. He was worth one billion, eight hundred millions of dollars – coins like you have there in your pouch, Edwin. And then came the Scarlet Death, and his wife became the wife of Bill, the first Chauffeur. He used to beat her, too. I have seen it myself.'

Hoo-Hoo, lying on his stomach and idly digging his toes in the sand, cried out and investigated, first his toe-nail, and next the small hole he had dug. The other two boys joined him, excavating the sand rapidly with their hands till there lay three skeletons exposed. Two were of adults, the third being that of a part-grown child. The old man hudged along on the ground and peered at the find.

'Plague victims,' he announced. 'That's the way they died everywhere in the last days. This must have been a family, running away from the contagion and perishing here on the Cliff House beach. They – what are you doing, Edwin?'

This question was asked in sudden dismay, as Edwin, using the back of his hunting-knife, began to knock out the teeth from the jaws of one of the skulls.

'Going to string 'em,' was the response.

The three boys were now hard at it; and quite a knocking and hammering rose, in which Granser babbled on unnoticed.

'You are true savages. Already has begun the custom of wearing human teeth. In another generation you will be perforating your noses and ears and wearing ornaments of bone and shell. I know. The human race is doomed to sink back farther and farther into the primitive night ere again it begins its bloody climb upward to civilization. When we increase and feel the lack of room, we will proceed to kill one another. And then I suppose you will wear human scalplocks at your waist, as well – as you, Edwin, who are the gentlest of my grandsons, have already begun with that vile pig tail. Throw it away, Edwin, boy; throw it away.'

'What a gabble the old geezer makes,' Hare-Lip remarked, when, the teeth all extracted, they began an attempt at equal division.

They were very quick and abrupt in their actions, and their speech, in moments of hot discussion over the allotment of the choicer teeth, was truly a gabble. They spoke in monosyllables and short jerky sentences that were more a gibberish than a language. And yet, through it ran hints of grammatical construction, and appeared vestiges of the conjugation of some superior culture. Even the speech of Granser was so corrupt that were it put down literally it would be almost so much nonsense to the reader. This, however, was when he talked with the boys. When he got into the full swing of babbling to himself, it slowly purged itself into pure English. The sentences grew longer and were enunciated with a rhythm and ease that was reminiscent of the lecture platform.

'Tell us about the Red Death, Granser,' Hare-Lip demanded, when the teeth affair had been satisfactorily concluded.

'The Scarlet Death,' Edwin corrected.

'An' don't work all that funny lingo on us,' Hare-Lip went on. 'Talk sensible, Granser, like a Santa Rosan ought to talk. Other Santa Rosans don't talk like you.'

CHAPTER TWO

The old man showed pleasure in being thus called upon. He cleared his throat and began.

'Twenty or thirty years ago my story was in great demand. But in these days nobody seems interested——'

'There you go!' Hare-Lip cried hotly. 'Cut out the funny stuff and talk sensible. What's *interested*? You talk like a baby that don't know how.'

'Let him alone,' Edwin urged, 'or he'll get mad and won't talk at all. Skip the funny places. We'll catch on to some of what he tells us.'

'Let her go, Granser,' Hoo-Hoo encouraged; for the old man was already maundering about the disrespect for elders and the reversion to cruelty of all humans that fell from high culture to primitive conditions.

The tale began.

'There were very many people in the world in those days. San Francisco alone held four millions——'

'What is millions?' Edwin interrupted.

Granser looked at him kindly.

'I know you cannot count beyond ten, so I will tell you. Hold up your two hands. On both of them you have altogether ten fingers and thumbs. Very well. I now take this grain of sand – you hold it, Hoo-Hoo.' He dropped the grain of sand into the lad's palm and went on. 'Now that grain of sand stands for the ten fingers of Edwin. I add another grain. That's ten more fingers. And I add another, and another, and another, until I have added as many grains as Edwin has fingers and thumbs. That makes what I call one hundred. Remember that word – one hundred. Now I put this pebble in Hare-Lip's hand. It stands for ten grains of sand, or ten tens of fingers, or one hundred fingers. I put in ten pebbles. They stand for a thousand fingers. I take a mussel-shell, and it stands for ten pebbles, or one hundred grains of sand, or one thousand fingers . . . '

And so on, laboriously, and with much reiteration, he strove to build up in their minds a crude conception of numbers. As the quantities increased, he had the boys holding different magnitudes in each of their hands. For still higher sums, he laid the symbols on the log of driftwood; and for symbols he was hard put being compelled to use the teeth from the skulls for millions, and the crab-shells for billions. It was here that he stopped, for the boys were showing signs of becoming tired.

'There were four million people in San Francisco – four teeth.'

The boys' eyes ranged along from the teeth and from hand to hand, down through the pebbles and sand-grains to Edwin's fingers. And back again they ranged along the ascending series in the effort to grasp such inconceivable numbers.

'That was a lot of folks, Granser,' Edwin at last hazarded.

'Like sand on the beach here, like sand on the beach, each grain of sand a man, or woman, or child. Yes, my boy, all those people lived right here in San Francisco. And at one time or another all those people came out on this very beach – more people than there are grains of sand. More – more – more. And San Francisco was a noble city. And across the bay – where we camped last year, even more people lived, clear from Point Richmond, on the level ground and on the hills, all the way around to San Leandro – one great city of seven million people. – Seven teeth . . . there, that's it, seven millions.'

Again the boys' eyes ranged up and down from Edwin's fingers to the teeth on the log.

'The world was full of people. The census of 2010 gave eight billions for the whole world – eight crab-shells, yes, eight billions. It was not like today. Mankind knew a great deal more about getting food. And the more food there was, the more people there were. In the year 1800, there were one hundred and seventy millions in Europe alone. One hundred years later – a grain of sand, Hoo-Hoo – one hundred years later, in 1900, there were five hundred millions in Europe – five grains of sand, Hoo-Hoo, and this one tooth. This shows how easy was the getting of food, and how men increased. And in the year 2000, there were fifteen hundred millions in Europe. And it was the same all over the rest of the world. Eight crab-shells there, yes, eight billion people were alive on the earth when the Scarlet Death began.

'I was a young man when the Plague came – twenty-seven years old; and I lived on the other side of San Francisco Bay, in Berkeley. You remember those great stone houses, Edwin, when we came down the hills from Contra Costa? That was where I lived, in those stone houses. I was a professor of English literature.'

Much of this was over the heads of the boys, but they strove to comprehend dimly this tale of the past.

'What was them stone houses for?' Hare-Lip queried.

'You remember when your dad taught you to swim?' The boy nodded. 'Well, in the University of California – that is the name we had for the houses – we taught young men and women how to think, just as I have taught you now, by sand and pebbles and shells, to know how many people lived in those days. There was very much to teach. The young men and women we taught were called students. We had large rooms in which we taught. I talked to them, forty or fifty at a time, just as I am talking to you now. I told them about the books other men had written before their time, and even, sometimes in their time——'

'Was that all you did – just talk, talk, talk?' Hoo-Hoo demanded. 'Who hunted your meat for you? and milked the goats? and caught the fish?'

'A sensible question, Hoo-Hoo, a sensible question. As I have told you, in those days food-getting was easy. We were very wise. A few men got the food for many men. The other men did other things. As you say I talked. I talked all the time, and for this food was given me – much food, fine food, beautiful food, food that I have not tasted in sixty years and shall never taste again. I sometimes think the most wonderful achievement of our tremendous civilization was food – its inconceivable abundance, its infinite variety, its marvellous delicacy. Oh, my grandsons, life was life in those days when we had such wonderful things to eat.'

This was beyond the boys, and they let it slip by, words and thoughts, as a mere senile wandering in the narrative.

'Our food-getters were called *freemen*. This was a joke. We of the ruling classes owned all the land, all the machines, all the food they got, and left them a little so that they might eat, and work and get us more food——'

'I'd have gone into the forest and got food for myself,' Hare-Lip announced; 'and if any man tried to take it away from me, I'd have killed him.'

The old man laughed.

'Did I not tell you that we of the ruling class owned all the land, all the forest, everything? Any food-getter who would not get food for us, him we punished or compelled to starve to death. And very few did that. They preferred to get food for us and make clothes for us and prepare and administer to us a thousand – a mussel-shell, Hoo-Hoo – a thousand satisfactions and delights. And I was Professor Smith in those days – Professor James Howard Smith. And my lecture courses were very popular – that is, very many of the young men and women liked to hear me talk about the books other men had written.

'And I was very happy, and I had beautiful things to eat. And my hands were soft, because I did no work with them, and my body was clean all over and dressed in the softest garments——' He surveyed his mangy goat-skin with disgust. 'We did not wear such things in those days. Even the slaves had better garments. And we were most clean. We washed our faces and hands often every day. You boys never wash unless you fall into the water or go in swimming.'

'Neither do you, Granser,' Hoo-Hoo retorted.

'I know, I know. I am a filthy old man. But times have changed. Nobody washes these days, and there are no conveniences. It is sixty years since I have seen a piece of soap. You do not know what soap is, and I shall not tell you, for I am telling the story of the Scarlet Death. You know what sickness is. We called it a disease. Very many of the diseases came from what we called germs. Remember that word – germs. A germ is a very small thing. It is like a woodtick, such as you find on the dogs in the spring of the year when they run in the forest. Only the germ is very small. It is so small that you cannot see it——'

Hoo-Hoo began to laugh.

'You're a queer un, Granser, talking about things you can't see. If you can't see 'em, how do you know they are? That's what I want to know. How do you know anything you can't see?'

'A good question, a very good question, Hoo-Hoo. But we did see – some of them. We had what we called microscopes and ultramicroscopes, and we put them to our eyes and looked through them, so that we saw things larger than they really were, and many things we could not see without the microscopes at all. Our best ultramicroscopes could make a germ look forty thousand times larger. A mussel-shell is a thousand fingers like Edwin's. Take forty mussel-shells, and by as many times larger was the germ when we looked at it through a microscope. And after that, we had other ways, by using what we called moving pictures, of making the forty-thousand-times germ many, many thousand times larger still. And thus we saw all these things which our eyes of themselves could not see. Take a grain of sand. Break it into ten pieces. Take one piece and break it into ten. Break one of those pieces into ten, and one of those into ten, and one of those into ten, and one of those into ten, and do it all day, and maybe, by sunset, you will have a piece as small as one of the germs.'

The boys were openly incredulous. Hare-Lip sniffed and sneered and Hoo-Hoo snickered, until Edwin nudged them to be silent.

'The woodtick sucks the blood of the dog, but the germ, being so very small, goes right into the blood of the body, and there it has many children. In those days there would be as many as a billion – a crab-shell, please – as many as that crab-shell in one man's body. We called germs micro-organisms. When a few million, or a billion, of them were in a man, in all the blood of a man, he was sick. These germs were a disease. There were many different kinds of them – more different kinds than there are grains of sand on this beach. We knew only a few of the kinds.

The micro-organic world was an invisible world, a world we could not see, and we knew very little about it. Yet we did know something. There was the *Bacillus anthracis*; there was the *micrococcus*; there was the *Bacterium termo*, and the *Bacterium lactis* – that's what turns the goat milk sour even to this day, Hare-Lip; and there were *Schizo-mycetes* without end. And there were many others. . . . '

Here the old man launched into a disquisition on germs and their natures, using words and phrases of such extraordinary length and meaninglessness, that the boys grinned at one another and looked out over the deserted ocean till they forgot the old man was babbling on.

'But the Scarlet Death, Granser,' Edwin at last suggested.

Granser recollected himself, and with a start tore himself away from the rostrum of the lecture-hall, where, to another-world audience, he had been expounding the latest theory, sixty years gone, of germs and germ-diseases.

'Yes, yes, Edwin; I had forgotten. Sometimes the memory of the past is very strong upon me, and I forget that I am a dirty old man, clad in goat-skin, wandering with my savage grandsons who are goat-herds in the primeval wilderness. "The fleeting systems lapse like foam," and so lapsed our glorious, colossal civilization. I am Granser, a tired old man. I belong to the tribe of Santa Rosans. I married into that tribe. My sons and daughters married into the Chauffeurs, the Sacramentos, and the Palo-Altos. You, Hare-Lip, are of the Chauffeurs. You, Edwin, are of the Sacramentos. And you, Hoo-Hoo, are of the Palo-Altos. Your tribe takes its name from a town that was near the seat of another great institution of learning. It was called Stanford University. Yes, I remember now. It is perfectly clear. I was telling you of the Scarlet Death. Where was I in my story?'

'You was telling about germs, the things you can't see but which make men sick,' Edwin prompted.

'Yes, that's where I was. A man did not notice at first when only a few of these germs got into his body. But each germ broke in half and became two germs, and they kept doing this very rapidly so that in a short time there were many millions of them in the body. Then the man was sick. He had a disease, and the disease was named after the kind of germ that was in him. It might be measles, it might be influenza, it might be yellow fever; it might be any of thousands and thousands of kinds of diseases.

'Now this is the strange thing about these germs. There were always new ones coming to live in men's bodies. Long and long and long ago, when there were only a few men in the world, there were few diseases. But as men increased and lived closely together in great cities and civilizations, new diseases arose, new kinds of germs entered their bodies.

Thus were countless millions and billions of human beings killed. And the more thickly men packed together, the more terrible were the new diseases that came to be. Long before my time, in the middle ages, there was the Black Plague that swept across Europe. It swept across Europe many times. There was tuberculosis, that entered into men wherever they were thickly packed. A hundred years before my time there was the bubonic plague. And in Africa was the sleeping sickness. The bacteriologists fought all these sicknesses and destroyed them, just as you boys fight the wolves away from your goats, or squash the mosquitoes that light on you. The bacteriologists——'

'But, Granser, what is a what-you-call-it?' Edwin interrupted.

'You, Edwin, are a goat-herd. Your task is to watch the goats. You know a great deal about goats. A bacteriologist watches germs. That's his task, and he knows a great deal about them. So, as I was saying, the bacteriologists fought with the germs and destroyed them – sometimes. There was leprosy, a horrible disease. A hundred years before I was born, the bacteriologists discovered the germ of leprosy. They knew all about it. They made pictures of it. I have seen those pictures. But they never found a way to kill it. But in 1984, there was the Pantoblast Plague, a disease that broke out in a country called Brazil and that killed millions of people. But the bacteriologists found it out, and found the way to kill it, so that the Pantoblast Plague went no farther. They made what they called a serum, which they put into a man's body and which killed the pantoblast germs without killing the man. And in 1910, there was Pellagra, and also the hookworm. These were easily killed by the bacteriologists. But in 1947 there arose a new disease that had never been seen before. It got into the bodies of babies of only ten months old or less, and it made them unable to move their hands and feet, or to eat, or anything; and the bacteriologists were eleven years in discovering how to kill that particular germ and save the babies.

'In spite of all these diseases, and of all the new ones that continued to arise, there were more and more men in the world. This was because it was easy to get food. The easier it was to get food, the more men there were; the more men there were, the more thickly were they packed together on the earth; and the more thickly they were packed, the more new kinds of germs became diseases. There were warnings. Soldervetzsky, as early as 1929, told the bacteriologists that they had no guaranty against some new disease, a thousand times more deadly than any they knew, arising and killing by the hundreds of millions and even by the billion. You see, the micro-organic world remained a mystery to the end. They knew there was such a world, and that from time to time armies of new germs emerged from it to kill men. And that was all they knew about it. For all they knew, in that invisible micro-organic world there might be as many different kinds of germs as there are grains of sand on this beach. And also, in that same invisible world it might well be that new kinds of germs came to be. It might be there that life originated – the "abysmal fecundity," Soldervetzsky called it, applying the words of other men who had written before him . . . '

It was at this point that Hare-Lip rose to his feet, an expression of huge contempt on his face.

'Granser,' he announced, 'you make me sick with your gabble. Why don't you tell about the Red Death? If you ain't going to, say so, an' we'll start back for camp.'

The old man looked at him and silently began to cry. The weak tears of age rolled down his cheeks, and all the feebleness of his eighty-seven years showed in his grief-stricken countenance.

'Sit down,' Edwin counselled soothingly. 'Granser's all right. He's just gettin' to the Scarlet Death, ain't you, Granser? He's just goin' to tell us about it right now. Sit down, Hare-Lip. Go ahead, Granser.'

CHAPTER THREE

The old man wiped the tears away on his grimy knuckles and took up the tale in a tremulous, piping voice that soon strengthened as he got the swing of the narrative.

'It was in the summer of 2013 that the Plague came. I was twenty-seven years old, and well do I remember it. Wireless despatches——'

Hare-Lip spat loudly his disgust, and Granser hastened to make amends.

'We talked through the air in those days, thousands and thousands of miles. And the word came of a strange disease that had broken out in New York. There were seventeen millions of people living then in that noblest city of America. Nobody thought anything about the news. It was only a small thing. There had been only a few deaths. It seemed, though, that they had died very quickly, and that one of the first signs of the disease was the turning red of the face and all the body. Within twenty-four hours came the report of the first case in Chicago. And on the same day, it was made public that London, the greatest city in the world, next to Chicago, had been secretly fighting the plague for two weeks and censoring the news despatches – that is, not permitting the word to go forth to the rest of the world that London had the plague.

'It looked serious, but we in California, like everywhere else, were not alarmed. We were sure that the bacteriologists would find a way to overcome this new germ, just as they had overcome other germs in the past. But the trouble was the astonishing quickness with which this germ destroyed human beings, and the fact that it inevitably killed any human body it entered. No one ever recovered. There was the old Asiatic cholera, when you might eat dinner with a man in good health in the evening, and the next morning, if you got up early enough, you would see him being hauled by your window in the death-cart. But this new plague was quicker than that – much quicker. From the moment of the first signs of it, a man would be dead in an hour. Some lasted for several hours. Many died within ten or fifteen minutes of the appearance of the first signs.

'The heart began to beat faster and the heat of the body to increase. Then came the scarlet rash, spreading like wild-fire over the face and body. Most persons never noticed the increase in heat and heart-beat, and the first they knew was when the scarlet rash came out. Usually they had convulsions at the time of the appearance of the rash. But these convulsions did not last long and were not very severe. If one lived through them, he became perfectly quiet, and only did he feel a numbness swiftly creeping up his body from the feet. The heels became numb first, then the legs, and hips, and when the numbness reached as high as his heart he died. They did not rave or sleep. Their minds always remained cool and calm up to the moment their heart numbed and stopped. And another strange thing was the rapidity of decomposition. No sooner was a person dead than the body seemed to fall to pieces, to fly apart, to melt away even as you looked at it. That was one of the reasons the plague spread so rapidly. All the billions of germs in a corpse were so immediately released.

'And it was because of all this that the bacteriologists had so little chance in fighting the germs. They were killed in their laboratories even as they studied the germ of the Scarlet Death. They were heroes. As fast as they perished, others stepped forth and took their places. It was in London that they first isolated it. The news was telegraphed everywhere. Trask was the name of the man who succeeded in this, but within thirty hours he was dead. Then came the struggle in all the laboratories to find something that would kill the plague germs. All drugs failed. You see, the problem was to get a drug, or serum, that would kill the germs in the body and not kill the body. They tried to fight it with other germs, to put into the body of a sick man germs that were the enemies of the plague germs——'

'And you can't see these germ-things, Granser,' Hare-Lip objected, 'and here you gabble, gabble, gabble about them as if they was anything, when they're nothing at all. Anything you can't see, ain't, that's what. Fighting things that ain't with things that aint! They must have been all fools in them days. That's why they croaked. I ain't goin' to believe in such rot, I tell you that.'

Granser promptly began to weep, while Edwin hotly took up his defence.

'Look here, Hare-Lip, you believe in lots of things you can't see.'

Hare-Lip shook his head.

'You believe in dead men walking about. You never seen one dead man walk about.'

'I tell you I seen 'em last winter, when I was wolf-hunting with dad.'

'Well, you always spit when you cross running water,' Edwin challenged.

'That's to keep off bad luck,' was Hare-Lip's defence.

'You believe in bad luck?'

'Sure.'

'An' you ain't never seen bad luck,' Edwin concluded triumphantly. 'You're just as bad as Granser and his germs. You believe in what you don't see. Go on, Granser.'

Hare-Lip, crushed by this metaphysical defeat, remained silent, and the old man went on. Often and often, though this narrative must not be clogged by the details, was Granser's tale interrupted while the boys squabbled among themselves. Also, among themselves they kept up a constant, low-voiced exchange of explanation and conjecture, as they strove to follow the old man into his unknown and vanished world.

'The Scarlet Death broke out in San Francisco. The first death came on a Monday morning. By Thursday they were dying like flies in Oakland and San Francisco. They died everywhere – in their beds, at their work, walking along the street. It was on Tuesday that I saw my first death – Miss Collbran, one of my students, sitting right there before my eyes, in my lecture-room. I noticed her face while I was talking. It had suddenly turned scarlet. I ceased speaking and could only look at her, for the first fear of the plague was already on all of us and we knew that it had come. The young women screamed and ran out of the room. So did the young men run out, all but two. Miss Collbran's convulsions were very mild and lasted less than a minute. One of the young men fetched her a glass of water. She drank only a little of it, and cried out:

'"My feet! All sensation has left them."

'After a minute she said, "I have no feet. I am unaware that I have any feet. And my knees are cold. I can scarcely feel that I have knees."

'She lay on the floor, a bundle of notebooks under her head. And we could do nothing. The coldness and the numbness crept up past her hips to her heart, and when it reached her heart she was dead. In fifteen minutes, by the clock – I timed it – she was dead, there, in my own classroom, dead. And she was a very beautiful, strong, healthy young woman. And from the first sign of the plague to her death only fifteen minutes elapsed. That will show you how swift was the Scarlet Death.

'Yet in those few minutes I remained with the dying woman in my classroom, the alarm had spread over the university; and the students, by thousands, all of them, had deserted the lecture-rooms and laboratories. When I emerged, on my way to make my report to the President of the Faculty, I found the university deserted. Across the campus were several stragglers hurrying for their homes. Two of them were running.

'President Hoag I found in his office, all alone, looking very old and very grey, with a multitude of wrinkles in his face that I had never seen before. At the sight of me, he pulled himself to his feet and tottered away to the inner office, banging the door after him and locking it. You see, he knew I had been exposed, and he was afraid. He shouted to me through the door to go away. I shall never forget my feelings as I walked down the silent corridors and out across that deserted campus. I was not afraid. I had been exposed, and I looked upon myself as already dead. It was not that, but a feeling of awful depression that impressed me. Everything had stopped. It was like the end of the world to me – my world. I had been born within sight and sound of the university. It had been my predestined career. My father had been a professor there before me, and his father before him. For a century and a half had this university, like a splendid machine, been running steadily on. And now in an instant, it had stopped. It was like seeing the sacred flame die down on some thrice-sacred altar. I was shocked, unutterably shocked.

'When I arrived home, my housekeeper screamed as I entered, and fled away. And when I rang, I found the house-maid had likewise fled. I investigated. In the kitchen I found the cook on the point of departure. But she screamed, too, and in her haste dropped a suitcase of her personal belongings and ran out of the house and across the grounds still screaming. I can hear her screams to this day. You see, we did not act in this way when ordinary diseases smote us. We were always calm over such things and sent for the doctors and nurses who knew just what to do. But this was different. It struck so suddenly, and killed so swiftly, and never missed a stroke. When the scarlet rash appeared on a person's face, that person was marked by death. There was never a known case of a recovery.

'I was alone in my big house. As I have told you often before, in those days we could talk with one another over wires or through the air. The telephone bell rang, and I found my brother talking to me. He told me that he was not coming home for fear of catching the plague from me, and that he had taken our two sisters to stop at Professor Bacon's home. He advised me to remain where I was, and wait to find out whether or not I had caught the plague.

'To all of this I agreed, staying in my house and for the first time in my life attempting to cook. And the plague did not come out on me. By means of the telephone I could talk with whomsoever I pleased and get the news. Also, there were the newspapers, and I ordered all of them to be thrown up to my door so that I could know what was happening with the rest of the world.

'New York City and Chicago were in chaos. And what happened with them was happening in all the large cities. A third of New York police were dead. Their chief was also dead, likewise the mayor. All law and order had ceased. The bodies were lying in the streets unburied. All railroads and vessels carrying food and such things into the great city had ceased running, and mobs of the hungry poor were pillaging the stores and warehouses. Murder and robbery and drunkenness were everywhere. Already the people had fled from the city by millions – at first the rich, in their private motor-cars and dirigibles, and then the great mass of the population, on foot, carrying the plague with them, themselves starving and pillaging the farmers and all the towns and villages on the way.

'The man who sent this news, the wireless operator, was alone with his instrument on the top of a lofty building. The people remaining in the city – he estimated them at several hundred thousand – had gone mad from fear and drink, and on all sides of him great fires were raging. He was a hero, that man who stayed by his post – an obscure newspaper man, most likely.

'For twenty-four hours, he said, no transatlantic airships had arrived and no more messages were coming from England. He did state, though, that a message from Berlin – that's in Germany – announced that Hoffmeyer, a bacteriologist of the Metchnikoff School, had discovered the serum for the plague. That was the last word, to this day, that we of America ever received from Europe. If Hoffmeyer discovered the serum, it was too late, or otherwise, long ere this, explorers from Europe would have come looking for us. We can only conclude that what happened in America happened in Europe, and that, at the best, some several score may have survived the Scarlet Death on that whole continent.

'For one day longer the despatches continued to come from New York. Then they, too, ceased. The man who had sent them, perched in his lofty building, had either died of the plague or been consumed in the great conflagrations he had described as raging around him. And what had occurred in New York had been duplicated in all the other cities. It was the same in San Francisco, and Oakland, and Berkeley. By Thursday the people were dying so rapidly that their corpses could not be handled and dead bodies lay everywhere. Thursday night the panic outrush for the country began. Imagine, my grandsons, people, thicker than the salmon-run you have seen on the Sacramento river, pouring out of the cities by millions, madly over the country, in vain attempt to escape the ubiquitous death. You see, they carried the germs with them. Even the airships of the rich, fleeing for mountain and desert fastnesses, carried the germs.

'Hundreds of these airships escaped to Hawaii, and not only did they bring the plague with them, but they found the plague already there before them. This we learned by the despatches, until all order in San Francisco vanished, and there were no operators left at their posts to receive or send. It was amazing, astounding, this loss of communication with the world. It was exactly as if the world had ceased, been blotted out. For sixty years that world has no longer existed for me. I know there must be such places as New York, Europe, Asia, and Africa; but not one word has been heard of them – not in sixty years. With the coming of the Scarlet Death the world fell apart, absolutely, irretrievably. Ten thousand years of culture and civilization passed in the twinkling of an eye, "lapsed like foam."

'I was telling about the airships of the rich. They carried the plague with them, and no matter where they fled, they died. I never encountered but one survivor of any of them – Mungerson. He was afterwards a Santa Rosan, and he married my eldest daughter. He came into the tribe eight years after the plague. He was then nineteen years old, and he was compelled to wait twelve years more before he could marry. You see, there were no unmarried women, and some of the older daughters of the Santa Rosans were already bespoken. So he was forced to wait until my Mary had grown to sixteen years. It was his son, Gimp-Leg, who was killed last year by the mountain lion.

'Mungerson was eleven years old at the time of the plague. His father was one of the Industrial Magnates, a very wealthy, powerful man. It was on his airship, the Condor, that they were fleeing, with all the family, for the wilds of British Columbia, which is far to the north of here. But there was some accident, and they were wrecked near Mount Shasta. You have heard of that mountain. It is far to the north. The plague broke out amongst them, and this boy of eleven was the only survivor. For eight years he was alone, wandering over a deserted land and looking vainly for his own kind. And at last, travelling south he picked up with us, the Santa Rosans.

'But I am ahead of my story. When the great exodus from the cities around San Francisco Bay began, and while the telephones were still working, I talked with my brother. I told him this flight from the cities was insanity, that there were no symptoms of the plague in me, and that the thing for us to do was to isolate ourselves and our relatives in some safe place. We decided on the Chemistry Building, at the university, and we planned to lay in a supply of provisions, and by force of arms to prevent any other persons from forcing their presence upon us after we had retired to our refuge.

'All this being arranged, my brother begged me to stay in my own house for at least twenty-four hours more, on the chance of the plague developing in me. To this I agreed, and he promised to come for me next day. We talked on over the details of the provisioning and the defending of the Chemistry Building until the telephone died. It died in the midst of our conversation. That evening there were no electric lights, and I was alone in my house in the darkness. No more newspapers were being printed, so I had no knowledge of what was taking place outside. I heard sound of rioting and pistol shots, and from my windows I could see the glare in the sky of some conflagration in the direction of Oakland. It was a night of terror. I did not sleep a wink. A man – why and how I do not know – was killed on the sidewalk in front of the house. I heard the rapid reports of an automatic pistol, and a few minutes later the wounded wretch crawled up to my door, moaning and crying out for help. Arming myself with two automatics, I went to him. By the light of a match I ascertained that while he was dying of the bullet wounds, at the same time the plague was on him. I fled indoors, whence I heard him moan and cry out for half an hour longer.

'In the morning, my brother came to me. I had gathered into a handbag what things of value I purposed taking, but when I saw his face I knew that he would never accompany me to the Chemistry Building. The plague was on him. He intended shaking my hand, but I went back hurriedly before him.

'"Look at yourself in the mirror", I commanded.

'He did so, and at the sight of his scarlet face, the colour deepening as he looked at it, he sank down nervously in a chair.

'"My God!" he said. "I've got it. Don't come near me. I am a dead man."

'Then the convulsions seized him. He was two hours in dying, and he was conscious to the last, complaining about the coldness and loss of sensation in his feet, his calves, his thighs, until at last it was his heart, and he was dead.

'That was the way the Scarlet Death slew. I caught up my handbag and fled. The sights in the streets were terrible. One stumbled on bodies everywhere. Some were not yet dead. And even as you looked, you saw men sink down with the death fastened upon them. There were numerous fires burning in Berkeley, while Oakland and San Francisco were apparently being swept by vast conflagrations. The smoke of the burning filled the heavens, so that the midday was as a gloomy twilight, and, in the shifts of wind, sometimes the sun shone through dimly, a dull red orb. Truly, my grandsons, it was like the last days of the end of the world.

'There were numerous stalled motor-cars, showing that the gasolene and the engine supplies of the garages had given out. I remember one such car. A man and woman lay back dead in the seats, and on the pavement near it were two more women and a child. Strange and terrible sights there were on every hand. People slipped by silently, furtively, like ghosts – white-faced women carrying infants in their arms; fathers leading children by the hand; singly, and in couples, and in families – all fleeing out of the city of death. Some carried supplies of food, others blankets and valuables, and there were many who carried nothing.

'There was a grocery store – a place where food was sold. The man to whom it belonged – I knew him well – a quiet, sober, but stupid and obstinate fellow, was defending it. The windows and doors had been broken in, but he, inside, hiding behind a counter, was discharging his pistol at a number of men on the sidewalk who were breaking in. In the entrance were several bodies – of men, I decided, whom he had killed earlier in the day. Even as I looked on from a distance, I saw one of the robbers break the windows of the adjoining store, a place where shoes were sold, and deliberately, set fire to it. I did not go to the groceryman's assistance. The time for such acts had already passed. Civilization was crumbling, and it was each for himself.'

CHAPTER FOUR

'I went away hastily, down a cross-street, and at the first corner I saw another tragedy. Two men of the working class had caught a man and a woman with two children, and were robbing them. I knew the man by sight, though I had never been introduced to him. He was a poet whose verses I had long admired. Yet I did not go to his help, for at the moment I came upon the scene there was a pistol shot, and I saw him sinking to the ground. The woman screamed, and she was felled with a fist-blow by one of the brutes. I cried out threateningly, whereupon they discharged their pistols at me, and I ran away around the corner. Here I was blocked by an advancing conflagration. The buildings on both sides were burning, and the street was filled with smoke and flame. From somewhere in that murk came a woman's voice calling shrilly for help. But I did not go to her. A man's heart turned to iron amid such scenes, and one heard all too many appeals for help.

'Returning to the corner, I found the two robbers were gone. The poet and his wife lay dead on the pavement. It was a shocking sight. The two children had vanished – whither I could not tell. And I knew, now, why it was that the fleeing persons I encountered slipped along so furtively and with such white faces. In the midst of our civilization, down in our slums and labour ghettoes, we had bred a race of barbarians, of savages; and now, in the time of our calamity, they turned upon us like the wild beasts they were and destroyed us. And they destroyed themselves as well. They inflamed themselves with strong drink and committed a thousand atrocities, quarrelling, and killing one another in the general madness. One group of working men I saw, of the better sort, who had banded together, and, with their women and children in their midst, the sick and aged in litters and being carried, and with a number of horses pulling a truck-load of provisions, they were fighting their way out of the city. They made a fine spectacle as they came down the street through the drifting smoke, though they nearly shot me when I first appeared in their path. As they went by, one of their leaders shouted out to me in apologetic explanation. He said they were killing the robbers and looters on sight, and that they had thus banded together as the only means by which to escape the prowlers.

'It was here that I saw for the first time what I was soon to see so often. One of the marching men had suddenly shown the unmistakable mark of the plague. Immediately those about him drew away, and he, without a remonstrance, stepped out of his place to let them pass on. A woman, most probably his wife, attempted to follow him. She was leading a little boy by the hand. But the husband commanded her sternly to go on, while others laid hands on her and restrained her from following him. This I saw, and I saw the man also, with his scarlet blaze of face, step into a doorway on the opposite side of the street. I heard the report of his pistol, and saw him sink lifeless to the ground.

'After being turned aside twice again by advancing fires, I succeeded in getting through to the university. On the edge of the campus I came upon a party of university folk who were going in the direction of the Chemistry Building. They were all family men, and their families were with them, including the nurses and the servants. Professor Badminton greeted me, and I had difficulty in recognizing him. Somewhere he had gone through flames, and his beard was singed off. About his head was a bloody bandage, and his clothes were filthy. He told me he had been cruelly beaten by prowlers, and that his brother had been killed the previous night, in the defence of their dwelling.

'Midway across the campus, he pointed suddenly to Mrs Swinton's face. The unmistakable scarlet was there. Immediately all the other women set up a screaming, and began to run away from her. Her two children were with a nurse, and these also ran with the women. But her husband, Doctor Swinton, remained with her.

'"Go on, Smith", he told me. "Keep an eye on the children. As for me, I shall stay with my wife. I know she is as already dead, but I can't leave her. Afterwards, if I escape, I shall come to the Chemistry Building, and do you watch for me and let me in."

'I left him bending over his wife and soothing her last moments, while I ran to overtake the party. We were the last to be admitted to the Chemistry Building. After that, with our automatic rifles we maintained our isolation. By our plans, we had arranged for a company of sixty to be in this refuge. Instead, every one of the number originally planned had added relatives and friends and whole families until there were over four hundred souls. But the Chemistry Building was large, and standing by itself, was in no danger of being burned by the great fires that raged everywhere in the city.

'A large quantity of provisions had been gathered, and a food committee took charge of it, issuing rations daily to the various families and groups that arranged themselves into messes. A number of committees were appointed, and we developed a very efficient organization: I was on the committee of defence, though for the first day no prowlers came near. We could see them in the distance, however, and by the smoke of their fires knew that several camps of them were occupying the far edge of the campus. Drunkenness was rife, and often we heard them singing ribald songs or insanely shouting. While the world crashed to ruin about them and all the air was filled with smoke of its burning, these low creatures gave a rein to their bestiality and fought and drank and died. And after all, what did it matter? Everybody died anyway, the good and the bad, the efficients and the weaklings, those that loved to live and those that scorned to live. They passed. Everything passed.

'When twenty-four hours had gone by and no signs of the plague were apparent, we congratulated ourselves and set about digging a well. You have seen the great iron pipes which in those days carried water to all the city-dwellers. We feared that the fires in the city would burst the pipes and empty the reservoirs. So we tore up the cement floor of the central court of the Chemistry Building and dug a well. There were many young men, undergraduates, with us, and we worked night and day on the well. And our fears were confirmed. Three hours before we reached water, the pipes went dry.

'A second twenty-four hours passed, and still the plague did not appear among us. We thought we were saved. But we did not know what I afterwards decided to be true, namely, that the period of the incubation of the plague germs in a human's body was a matter of a number of days. It slew so swiftly when once it manifested itself, that we were led to believe that the period of incubation was equally swift. So, when two days had left us unscathed, we were elated with the idea that we were free of the contagion.

'But the third day disillusioned us. I can never forget the night preceding it. I had charge of the night guards from eight to twelve, and from the roof of the building I watched the passing of all man's glorious works. So terrible were the local conflagrations that all the sky was lighted up. One could read the finest print in the red glare. All the world seemed wrapped in flames. San Francisco spouted smoke and fire from a score of vast conflagrations that were like so many active volcanoes. Oakland, San Leandro, Haywards – all were burning; and to the northward, clear to Point Richmond, other fires were at work. It was an awe-inspiring spectacle. Civilization, my grandsons, civilization was passing in a sheet of flame and a breath of death. At ten o'clock that night, the great powder magazines at Point Pinole exploded in rapid succession. So terrific were the concussions that the strong building rocked as in an earthquake, while every pane of glass was broken. It was then that I left the roof and went down the long corridors, from room to room, quieting the alarmed women and telling them what had happened.

'An hour later, at a window on the ground floor, I heard pandemonium break out in the camps of the prowlers. There were cries and screams, and shots from many pistols. As we afterwards conjectured, this fight had been precipitated by an attempt on the part of those that were well to drive out those that were sick. At any rate, a number of the plague-stricken prowlers escaped across the campus and drifted against our doors. We warned them back, but they cursed us and discharged a fusillade from their pistols. Professor Merryweather, at one of the windows, was instantly killed, the bullet striking him squarely between the eyes. We opened fire in turn, and all the prowlers fled away with the exception of three. One was a woman. The plague was on them and they were reckless. Like foul fiends, there in the red glare from the skies, with faces blazing, they continued to curse us and fire at us. One of the men I shot with my own hand. After that the other man and the woman, still cursing us, lay down under our windows, where we were compelled to watch them die of the plague.

'The situation was critical. The explosions of the powder magazines had broken all the windows of the Chemistry Building, so that we were exposed to the germs from the corpses. The sanitary committee was called upon to act, and it responded nobly. Two men were required to go out and remove the corpses, and this meant the probable sacrifice of their own lives, for, having performed the task, they were not to be permitted to re-enter the building. One of the professors, who was a bachelor, and one of the undergraduates volunteered. They bade goodbye to us and went forth. They were heroes. They gave up their lives that four hundred others might live. After they had performed their work, they stood for a moment, at a distance, looking at us wistfully. Then they waved their hands in farewell and went slowly across the campus toward the burning city.

'And yet it was useless. The next morning the first one of us was smitten with the plague – a little nurse-girl in the family of Professor Stout. It was no time for weak-kneed, sentimental policies. On the chance that she might be the only one, we thrust her forth from the building and commanded her to be gone. She went away slowly across the campus, wringing her hands and crying pitifully. We felt like brutes, but what were we to do? There were four hundred of us, and individuals had to be sacrificed.

'In one of the laboratories three families had domiciled themselves, and that afternoon we found among them no less than four corpses and seven cases of the plague in all its different stages.

'Then it was that the horror began. Leaving the dead where they had fallen, we forced the living ones to segregate themselves in another room. The plague began to break out among the rest of us and as fast as the symptoms appeared, we sent the stricken ones to these segregated rooms. We compelled them to walk there by themselves, so as to avoid laying hands on them. It was heartrending. But still the plague raged among us, and room after room was filled with the dead and dying. And so we who were yet clean retreated to the next floor and to the next, before this sea of the dead, that, room by room and floor by floor, inundated the building.

'The place became a charnel house, and in the middle of the night the survivors fled forth, taking nothing with them except arms and ammunition and a heavy store of tinned foods. We camped on the opposite side of the campus from the prowlers, and, while some stood guard, others of us volunteered to scout into the city in quest of horse, motor-cars, carts, and wagons, or anything that would carry our provisions and enable us to emulate the banded working men I had seen fighting their way out to the open country.

'I was one of these scouts; and Doctor Hoyle, remembering that his motor-car had been left behind in his home garage, told me to look for it. We scouted in pairs, and Dombey, a young undergraduate, accompanied me. We had to cross half a mile of the residence portion of the city to get to Doctor Hoyle's home. Here the buildings stood apart, in the midst of trees and grassy lawns, and here the fires had played freaks, burning whole blocks, skipping blocks, and often skipping a single house in a block. And here, too, the prowlers were still at their work. We carried our automatic pistols openly in our hands, and looked desperate enough, forsooth, to keep them from attacking us. But at Doctor Hoyle's house the thing happened. Untouched by fire, even as we came to it the smoke of flames burst forth.

'The miscreant who had set fire to it staggered down the steps and out along the driveway. Sticking out of his coat pockets were bottles of whisky, and he was very drunk. My first impulse was to shoot him, and I have never ceased regretting that I did not. Staggering and maundering to himself, with bloodshot eyes, and a raw bleeding slash down one side of his bewhiskered face, he was altogether the most nauseating specimen of degradation and filth I had ever encountered. I did not shoot him, and he leaned against a tree on the lawn to let us go by. Just as we were opposite him, he suddenly drew a pistol and shot Dombey through the head. It was the most absolute, wanton act. The next instant I shot him. But it was too late. Dombey expired without a groan, immediately. I doubt if he ever knew what had happened to him.

'Leaving the two corpses, I hurried on past the burning house to the garage, and there found Doctor Hoyle's motor-car. The tanks were filled with gasolene, and it was ready for use. And it was in this car that I threaded the streets of the ruined city and came back to the survivors on the campus. The other scouts returned, but none had been so fortunate. Professor Fairmead had found a Shetland pony, but the poor creature, tied in a stable and abandoned for days, was so weak from want of food and water that it could carry no burden at all. Some of them were for turning it loose, but I insisted that we should lead it along with us, so that, if we got out of food, we would have it to eat.

'There were forty-seven of us when we started, many being women and children. The President of the Faculty, an old man to begin with, and now hopelessly broken by the awful happenings of the past week, rode in the motor-car with several young children and the aged mother of Professor Fairmead. Wathope, a young professor of English, who had a grievous bullet-wound in his leg drove the car. The rest of us walked, Professor Fairmead leading the pony.

'It was what should have been a bright summer day, but the smoke from the burning world filled the sky, through which the sun shone murkily, a dull and lifeless orb, blood-red and ominous. But we had grown accustomed to that blood-red sun. With the smoke it was different. It bit into our nostrils and eyes, and there was not one of us whose eyes were not bloodshot. We directed our course to the south-east through the endless miles of suburban residences, travelling along where the first swells of low hills rose from the flat of the central city. It was by this way, only, that we could expect to gain the country.

Our progress was painfully slow. The women and children could not walk fast. They did not dream of walking, my grandsons, in the way all people walk today. In truth, none of us knew how to walk. It was not until after the plague that I learned really to walk. So it was that the pace of the slowest was the pace of all, for we dared not separate on account of the prowlers. There were not so many now of these human beasts of prey. The plague had already well diminished their numbers, but enough still lived to be a constant menace to us. Many of the beautiful residences were untouched by fire, yet smoking ruins were everywhere. The prowlers, too, seemed to have got over their insensate desire to burn, and it was more rarely that we saw houses freshly on fire.

'Several of us scouted among the private garages in search of motor-cars and gasolene. But in this we were unsuccessful. The first great flights from the cities had swept all such utilities away. Calgan, a fine young man, was lost in this work. He was shot by prowlers while crossing a lawn. Yet this was our only casualty, though, once, a drunken brute deliberately opened fire on all of us. Luckily, he fired wildly and we shot him before he had done any hurt.

'At Fruitvale, still in the heart of the magnificent residence section of the city, the plague again smote us. Professor Fairmead was the victim. Making signs to us that his mother was not to know, he turned aside into the grounds of a beautiful mansion. He sat down forlornly on the steps of the front veranda, and I, having lingered, waved him a last farewell. That night, several miles beyond Fruitvale and still in the city, we made camp. And that night we shifted camp twice to get away from our dead. In the morning there were thirty of us. I shall never forget the President of the Faculty. During the morning's march his wife, who was walking, betrayed the fatal symptoms, and when she drew aside to let us go on, he insisted on leaving the motor-car and remaining with her. There was quite a discussion about this, but in the end we gave in. It was just as well, for we knew not which ones of us, if any, might ultimately escape.

'That night, the second of our march, we camped beyond Haywards in the first stretches of country. And in the morning there were eleven of us that lived. Also, during the night, Wathope, the professor with the wounded leg, deserted us in the motor-car. He took with him his sister and his mother and most of our tinned provisions. It was that day, in the afternoon, while resting by the wayside, that I saw the last airship I shall ever see. The smoke was much thinner here in the country, and I first sighted the ship drifting and veering helplessly at an elevation of two thousand feet. What had happened I could not conjecture, but even as we looked we saw her bow dip down lower and lower. Then the bulkheads of the various gas-chambers must have burst, for, quite perpendicular, she fell like a plummet to the earth. And from that day to this I have not seen another airship. Often and often, during the next few years, I scanned the sky for them, hoping against hope that somewhere in the world civilization had survived. But it was not to be. What happened with us in California must have happened with everybody everywhere.

'Another day, and at Niles there were three of us. Beyond Niles, in the middle of the highway, we found Wathope. The motor-car had broken down, and there, on the rugs which they had spread on the ground, lay the bodies of his sister, his mother and himself.

'Wearied by the unusual exercise of continual walking, that night I slept heavily. In the morning I was alone in the world. Canfield and Parsons, my last companions, were dead of the plague. Of the four hundred that sought shelter in the Chemistry Building, and of the forty-seven that began the march, I alone remained – I and the Shetland pony. Why this should be so there is no explaining. I did not catch the plague, that is all. I was immune. I was merely the one lucky man in a million – just as every survivor was one in a million, or, rather, in several millions, for the proportion was at least that.'

CHAPTER FIVE

'For two days I sheltered in a pleasant grove where there had been no deaths. In those two days, while badly depressed and believing that my turn would come at any moment, nevertheless I rested and recuperated. So did the pony. And on the third day, putting what small store of tinned provisions I possessed on the pony's back, I started on across a very lonely land. Not a live man, woman, or child did I encounter, though the dead were everywhere. Food, however, was abundant. The land then was not as it is now. It was all cleared of trees and brush and it was cultivated. The food for millions of mouths was growing, ripening, and going to waste. From the fields and orchards I gathered vegetables, fruits, and berries. Around the deserted farmhouses I got eggs and caught chickens. And frequently I found supplies of tinned provisions in the store-rooms.

'A strange thing was what was taking place with all the domestic animals. Everywhere they were going wild and preying on one another. The chickens and ducks were the first to be destroyed, while the pigs were the first to go wild, followed by the cats. Nor were the dogs long in adapting themselves to the changed conditions. There was a veritable plague of dogs. They devoured the corpses, barked and howled during the nights, and in the daytime slunk about in the distance. As the time went by, I noticed a change in their behaviour. At first they were apart from one another, very suspicious and very prone to fight. But after a not very long while they began to come together and run in packs. The dog, you see, always was a social animal, and this was true before ever he came to be domesticated by man. In the last days of the world before the plague, there were many, many very different kinds of dogs – dogs without hair and dogs with warm fur, dogs so small that they would make scarcely a mouthful for other dogs that were as large as mountain lions. Well, all the small dogs, and the weak types, were killed by their fellows. Also, the very large ones were not adapted for the wild life and bred out. As a result, the many different kinds of dogs disappeared, and there remained, running in packs, the medium-sized wolfish dogs that you know to-day.'

'But the cats don't run in packs, Granser,' Hoo-Hoo objected.

'The cat was never a social animal. As one writer in the nineteenth century said, the cat walks by himself. He always walked by himself, from before the time he was tamed by man, down through the long ages of domestication, to to-day when once more he is wild.

'The horses also went wild, and all the fine breeds we had degenerated into the small mustang horse you know to-day. The cows likewise went wild, as did the pigeons and the sheep. And that a few of the chickens survived you know yourself. But the wild chicken of today is quite a different thing from the chickens we had in those days.

'But I must go on with my story. I travelled through a deserted land. As the time went by I began to yearn more and more for human beings. But I never found one, and I grew lonelier and lonelier. I crossed Livermore Valley and the mountains between it and the great valley of the San Joaquin. You have never seen that valley, but it is very large and it is the home of the wild horse. There are great droves there, thousands and tens of thousands. I revisited it thirty years after, so I know. You think there are lots of wild horses down here in the coast valleys, but these are as nothing compared with those of the San Joaquin. Strange to say, the cows, when they went wild, went back into the lower mountains. Evidently they were better able to protect themselves there.

'In the country districts, the ghouls and prowlers had been less in evidence, for I found many villages and towns untouched by fire. But they were filled by the pestilential dead, and I passed by without exploring them. It was near Lathrop that, out of my loneliness, I picked up a pair of collie dogs that were so newly free that they were urgently willing to return to their allegiance to man. These collies accompanied me for many years, and the strains of them are in those very dogs there that you boys have to-day. But in sixty years the collie strain has worked out. These brutes are more like domesticated wolves than anything else.'

Hare-Lip rose to his feet, glanced to see that the goats were safe, and looked at the sun's position in the afternoon sky, advertising impatience at the prolixity of the old man's tale. Urged to hurry by Edwin, Granser went on.

'There is little more to tell. With my two dogs and my pony, and riding a horse I had managed to capture, I crossed the San Joaquin and went on to a wonderful valley in the Sierras called Yosemite. In the great hotel there I found a prodigious supply of tinned provisions. The pasture was abundant, as was the game, and the river that ran through the valley was full of trout. I remained there three years in an utter loneliness that none but a man who has once been highly civilized can understand. Then I could stand it no more. I felt I was going crazy. Like the dog, I was a social animal and I needed my kind. I reasoned that since I had survived the plague, there was a possibility that others had survived. Also, I reasoned that after three years the plague germs must all be gone and the land be clean again.

'With my horse and dogs and pony, I set out. Again I crossed the San Joaquin Valley, the mountains beyond, and came down into Livermore Valley. The change in those three years was amazing. All the land had been splendidly tilled, and now I could scarcely recognize it, such was the sea of rank vegetation that had overrun the agricultural handiwork of man. You see, the wheat, the vegetables, and orchard trees had always been cared for and nursed by man, so that they were soft and tender. The weeds and wild bushes and such things, on the contrary, had always been fought by man, so that they were tough and resistant. As a result, when the hand of man was removed, the wild vegetation smothered and destroyed practically all the domesticated vegetation. The coyotes were greatly increased, and it was at this time that I first encountered wolves, straying in twos and threes and small packs down from the regions where they had always persisted.

'It was at Lake Temescal, not far from the one-time city of Oakland, that I came upon the first live human beings. Oh, my grandsons, how can I describe to you my emotion, when, astride my horse and dropping down the hillside to the lake, I saw the smoke of a camp-fire rising through the trees. Almost did my heart stop beating. I felt that I was going crazy. Then I heard the cry of a babe – a human babe. And dogs barked, and my dogs answered. I did not know but what I was the one human alive in the whole world. It could not be true that here were others – smoke, and the cry of a babe.

'Emerging on the lake, there, before my eyes, not a hundred yards away, I saw a man, a large man. He was standing on an outjutting rock and fishing. I was overcome. I stopped my horse. I tried to call out but could not. I waved my hand. It seemed to me that the man looked at me, but he did not appear to wave. Then I laid my head on my arms there in the saddle. I was afraid to look again, for I knew it was an hallucination, and I knew that if I looked the man would be gone. And so precious was the hallucination, that I wanted it to persist yet a little while. I knew, too, that as long as I did not look it would persist.

'Thus I remained until I heard my dogs snarling, and a man's voice. What do you think the voice said? I will tell you. It said: "*Where in hell did you come from?*"

'Those were the words, the exact words. That was what your other grandfather said to me, Hare-Lip, when he greeted me there on the shore of Lake Temescal fifty-seven years ago. And they were the most ineffable words I have ever heard. I opened my eyes, and there he stood before me, a large, dark, hairy man, heavy-jawed, slant-browed, fierce-eyed. How I got off my horse I do not know. But it seemed that the next I knew I was clasping his hand with both of mine and crying. I would have embraced him, but he was ever a narrow-minded, suspicious man, and he drew away from me. Yet did I cling to his hand and cry.'

Granser's voice faltered and broke at the recollection, and the weak tears streamed down his cheeks while the boys looked on and giggled.

'Yet did I cry,' he continued, 'and desire to embrace him, though the Chauffeur was a brute, a perfect brute – the most abhorrent man I have ever known. His name was . . . strange, how I have forgotten his name. Everybody called him Chauffeur – it was the name of his occupation, and it stuck. That is how, to this day, the tribe he founded is called the Chauffeur Tribe.

'He was a violent, unjust man. Why the plague spared him I can never understand. It would seem, in spite of our old metaphysical notions about absolute justice, that there is no justice in the universe. Why did he live? – an iniquitous, moral monster, a blot on the face of nature, a cruel, relentless, bestial cheat as well. All he could talk about was motor-cars, machinery, gasolene, and garages – and especially, and with huge delight, of his mean pilferings and sordid swindlings of the persons who had employed him in the days before the coming of the plague. And yet he was spared, while hundreds of millions, yea, billions of better men were destroyed.

'I went on with him to his camp, and there I saw her, Vesta, the one woman. It was glorious and . . . pitiful. There she was, Vesta Van Warden, the young wife of John Van Warden, clad in rags, with marred and scarred and oil-calloused hands, bending over the camp-fire and doing scullion work – she, Vesta, who had been born to the purple of the greatest baronage of wealth the world has ever known. John Van Warden, her husband, worth one billion, eight hundred millions and President of the Board of Industrial Magnates, had been the ruler of America. Also, sitting on the International Board of Control, he had been one of the seven men who ruled the world. And she herself had come of equally noble stock. Her father, Philip Saxon, had been President of the Board of Industrial Magnates up to the time of his death. The office was in process of becoming hereditary, and had Philip Saxon had a son, that son would have succeeded him. But his only child was Vesta, the perfect flower of generations of the highest culture this planet has ever produced. It was not until the engagement between Vesta and Van Warden took place that Saxon indicated the latter as his successor. It was, I am sure, a political marriage. I have reason to believe that Vesta never really loved her husband in the mad passionate way of which the poets used to sing. It was more like the marriages that obtained among crowned heads in the days before they were displaced by the Magnates.

'And there she was, boiling fish-chowder in a soot-covered pot, her glorious eyes inflamed by the acrid smoke of the open fire. Hers was a sad story. She was the one survivor in a million, as I had been, as the Chauffeur had been. On a crowning eminence of the Alameda Hills, overlooking San Francisco Bay, Van Warden had built a vast summer palace. It was surrounded by a park of a thousand acres. When the plague broke out, Van Warden sent her there. Armed guards patrolled the boundaries of the park, and nothing entered in the way of provisions or even mail matter that was not first fumigated. And yet did the plague enter, killing the guards at their posts, the servants at their tasks, sweeping away the whole army of retainers – or, at least, all of them who did not flee to die elsewhere. So it was that Vesta found herself the sole living person in the palace that had become a charnel house.

'Now the Chauffeur had been one of the servants that ran away. Returning, two months afterward, he discovered Vesta in a little summer pavilion where there had been no deaths and where she had established herself. He was a brute. She was afraid, and she ran away and hid among the trees. That night, on foot, she fled into the mountains – she, whose tender feet and delicate body had never known the bruise of stones nor the scratch of briars. He followed, and that night he caught her. He struck her. Do you understand? He beat her with those terrible fists of his and made her his slave. It was she who had to gather the firewood, build the fires, cook, and do all the degrading camp-labour – she, who had never performed a menial act in her life. These things he compelled her to do, while he, a proper savage, elected to lie around camp and look on. He did nothing, absolutely nothing, except on occasion to hunt meat or catch fish.'

'Good for Chauffeur,' Hare-Lip commented in an undertone to the other boys. 'I remember him before he died. He was a corker. But he did things, and he made things go. You know, Dad married his daughter, an' you ought to see the way he knocked the spots outa Dad. The Chauffeur was a son-of-a-gun. He made us kids stand around. Even when he was croakin', he reached out for me, once, an' laid my head open with that long stick he kept always beside him.'

Hare-Lip rubbed his bullet head reminiscently, and the boys returned to the old man, who was maundering ecstatically about Vesta, the squaw of the founder of the Chauffeur Tribe.

'And so I say to you that you cannot understand the awfulness of the situation. The Chauffeur was a servant, understand, a servant. And he cringed, with bowed head, to such as she. She was a lord of life, both by birth and by marriage. The destinies of millions, such as he, she carried in the hollow of her pink-white hand. And, in the days before the plague, the slightest contact with such as he would have been pollution. Oh, I have seen it. Once, I remember, there was Mrs Goldwin, wife of one of the great magnates. It was on a landing-stage, just as she was embarking in her private dirigible, that she dropped her parasol. A servant picked it up and made the mistake of handing it to her – to her, one of the greatest royal ladies of the land! She shrank back, as though he were a leper, and indicated her secretary to receive it. Also, she ordered her secretary to ascertain the creature's name and to see that he was immediately discharged from service. And such a woman was Vesta Van Warden. And her the Chauffeur beat and made his slave.

' . . . Bill – that was it; Bill, the Chauffeur. That was his name. He was a wretched, primitive man, wholly devoid of the finer instincts and chivalrous promptings of a cultured soul. No, there is no absolute justice, for him to fell that wonder of womanhood, Vesta Van Warden. The grievousness of this you will never understand, my grandsons; for you are yourselves primitive little savages, unaware of aught else but savagery. Why should Vesta not have been mine? I was a man of culture and refinement, a professor in a great university. Even so, in the time before the plague, such was her exalted position, she would not have deigned to know that I existed. Mark, then, the abysmal degradation to which she fell at the hands of the Chauffeur. Nothing less than the destruction of all mankind had made it possible that I should know her, look in her eyes, converse with her, touch her hand – ay, and love her and know that her feelings towards me were very kindly. I have reason to believe that she, even she, would have loved me, there being no other man in the world except the Chauffeur. Why when it destroyed eight billions of souls, did not the plague destroy just one more man, and that man the Chauffeur?

'Once, when the Chauffeur was away fishing, she begged me to kill him. With tears in her eyes she begged me to kill him. But he was a strong and violent man, and I was afraid. Afterwards, I talked with him. I offered him my horse, my pony, my dogs, all that I possessed, if he would give Vesta to me. And he grinned in my face and shook his head. He was very insulting. He said that in the old days he had been a servant, had been dirt under the feet of men like me and of women like Vesta, and that now he had the greatest lady in the land to be servant to him and cook his food and nurse his brats. "You had your day before the plague," he said; "but this is my day, and a damned good day it is. I wouldn't trade back to the old times for anything." Such words he spoke, but they are not his words. He was a vulgar, low-minded man, and vile oaths fell continually from his lips.

'Also, he told me that if he caught me making eyes at his woman, he'd wring my neck and give her a beating as well. What was I to do? I was afraid. He was a brute. That first night, when I discovered the camp, Vesta and I had great talk about the things of our vanished world. We talked of art, and books, and poetry; and the Chauffeur listened and grinned and sneered. He was bored and angered by our way of speech which he did not comprehend, and finally he spoke up and said: "And this is Vesta Van Warden, one-time wife of Van Warden the Magnate – a high and stuck-up beauty, who is now my squaw. Eh, Professor Smith, times is changed, times is changed. Here, you, woman, take off my mocassins, and lively about it. I want Professor Smith to see how well I have you trained."

'I saw her clench her teeth, and the flame of revolt rise in her face. He drew back his gnarled fist to strike, and I was afraid, and sick at heart. I could do nothing to prevail against him. So I got up to go, and not be a witness to such indignity. But the Chauffeur laughed and threatened me with a beating if I did not stay and behold. And I sat there, perforce, by the camp-fire on the shore of Lake Temescal, and saw Vesta, Vesta Van Warden, kneel and remove the mocassins of that grinning, hairy, ape-like human brute.

' . . . Oh, you do not understand, my grandsons. You have never known anything else, and you do not understand.

"'Halter-broke and bridle-wise", the Chauffeur gloated, while she performed that dreadful, menial task. "A trifle balky at times, Professor, a trifle balky; but a clout alongside the jaw makes her as meek and gentle as a lamb."

'And another time he said: "We've got to start all over and replenish the earth and multiply. You're handicapped, Professor. You ain't got no wife, and we're up against a regular Garden-of-Eden proposition. But I ain't proud. I'll tell you what, Professor." He pointed at their little infant, barely a year old. "There's your wife, though you'll have to wait till she grows up. It's rich ain't it? We're all equals here, and I'm the biggest toad in the splash. But I ain't stuck up – not I. I do you the honour, Professor Smith, the very great honour of betrothing to you my and Vesta Van Warden's daughter. Ain't it cussed bad that Van Warden ain't here to see.'"

CHAPTER SIX

'I lived three weeks of infinite torment there in the Chauffeur's camp. And then, one day, tiring of me, or of what to him was my bad effect on Vesta, he told me that the year before, wandering through the Contra

Costa Hills, to the Straits of Carquinez, across the Straits he had seen a smoke. This meant that there were still other human beings, and that for three weeks he had kept this inestimably precious information from me. I departed at once, with my dogs and horses, and journeyed across the Contra Costa Hills to the Straits. I saw no smoke on the other side, but at Port Costa discovered a small steel barge on which I was able to embark my animals. Old canvas which I found served me for a sail, and a southerly breeze fanned me across the Straits and up the ruins of Vallejo. Here, on the outskirts of the city, I found evidences of a recently occupied camp. Many clam shells showed me why these humans had come to the shores of the Bay. This was the Santa Rosa Tribe, and I followed its track along the old railroad right-of-way across the salt marshes to Sonoma Valley. Here, at the old brickyard at Glen Ellen, I came upon the camp. There were eighteen souls all told. Two were old men, one of whom was Jones, a banker. The other was Harrison, a retired pawn-broker, who had taken for wife the matron of the State Hospital for the Insane at Napa. Of all the persons of the city of Napa, and of all the other towns and villages in that rich and populous valley, she had been the only survivor. Next, there were the three young men – Cardiff and Hale, who had been farmers, and Wainwright, a common day-labourer. All three had found wives. To Hale, a crude, illiterate farmer, had fallen Isadore, the greatest prize, next to Vesta, of the women who came through the plague. She was one of the world's most noted singers, and the plague had caught her at San Francisco. She has talked with me for hours at a time telling me of her adventures, until, at last, rescued by Hale in the Mendocino Forest Reserve, there had remained nothing for her to do but to become his wife. But Hale was a good fellow, in spite of his illiteracy. He had a keen sense of justice and right-dealing, and she was far happier with him than was Vesta with the Chauffeur.

'The wives of Cardiff and Wainwright were ordinary women, accustomed to toil, with strong constitutions – just the type for the wild new life which they were compelled to live. In addition were two adult idiots from the feeble-minded home at Eldredge, and five or six young children and infants born after the formation of the Santa Rosa Tribe. Also, there was Bertha. She was a good woman, Hare-Lip, in spite of the sneers of your father. Her I took for wife. She was the mother of your father, Edwin, and of yours, Hoo-Hoo. And it was our daughter, Vera, who married your father, Hare-Lip – your father, Sandow, who was the oldest son of Vesta Van Warden and the Chauffeur.

'And so it was that I became the nineteenth member of the Santa Rosa Tribe. There were only two outsiders added after me. One was Mungerson, descended from the Magnates, who wandered alone in the wilds of Northern California for eight years before he came south and joined us. He it was who waited twelve years more before he married my daughter, Mary. The other was Johnson, the man who founded the Utah Tribe. That was where he came from, Utah, a country that lies very far away from here, across the great deserts, to the east. It was not until twenty-seven years after the plague that Johnson reached California. In all that Utah region he reported but three survivors, himself one, and all men. For many years these three men lived and hunted together, until, at last, desperate, fearing that with them the human race would perish utterly from the planet, they headed westward on the possibility of finding women survivors in California. Johnson alone came through the great desert, where his two companions died. He was forty-six years old when he joined us, and he married the fourth daughter of Isadore and Hale, and his eldest son married your aunt, Hare-Lip, who was the third daughter of Vesta and the Chauffeur. Johnson was a strong man, with a will of his own. And it was because of this that he seceded from the Santa Rosans and formed the Utah Tribe at San Jose. It is a small tribe – there are only nine in it; but, though he is dead, such was his influence and the strength of his breed, that it will grow into a strong tribe and play a leading part in the recivilization of the planet.

'There are only two other tribes that we know of – the Los Angelitos and the Carmelitos. The latter started from one man and woman. He was called Lopez, and he was descended from the ancient Mexicans and was very black. He was a cowherd in the ranges beyond Carmel, and his wife was a maidservant in the great Del Monte Hotel. It was seven years before we first got in touch with the Los Angelitos. They have a good country down there, but it is too warm. I estimate the present population of the world at between three hundred and fifty and four hundred – provided, of course, that there are no scattered little tribes elsewhere in the world. If there be such, we have not heard from them. Since Johnson crossed the desert from Utah, no word nor sign has come from the East or anywhere else. The great world which I knew in my boyhood and early manhood is gone. It has ceased to be. I am the last man who was alive in the days of the plague and who knows the wonders of that far-off time. We, who mastered the planet – its earth, and sea, and sky – and who were as very gods, now live in primitive savagery along the water courses of this California country.

'But we are increasing rapidly – your sister, Hare-Lip, already has four children. We are increasing rapidly and making ready for a new climb toward civilization. In time, pressure of population will compel us to spread out, and a hundred generations from now we may expect our descendants to start across the Sierras, oozing slowly along, generation by generation, over the great continent to the colonization of the East – a new Aryan drift around the world.

'But it will be slow, very slow; we have so far to climb. We fell so hopelessly far. If only one physicist or one chemist had survived! But it was not to be, and we have forgotten everything. The Chauffeur started working in iron. He made the forge which we use to this day. But he was a lazy man, and when he died he took with him all he knew of metals and machinery. What was I to know of such things? I was a classical scholar, not a chemist. The other men who survived were not educated. Only two things did the Chauffeur accomplish – the brewing of strong drink and the growing of tobacco. It was while he was drunk, once, that he killed Vesta. I firmly belive that he killed Vesta in a fit of drunken cruelty, though he always maintained that she fell into the lake and was drowned.

'And my grandsons, let me warn you against the medicine-men. They call themselves *doctors*, travestying what was once a noble profession, but in reality they are medicine-men, devil-devil men, and they make for superstition and darkness. They are cheats and liars. But so debased and degraded are we, that we believe their lies. They, too, will increase in numbers as we increase, and they will strive to rule us. Yet are they liars and charlatans. Look at young Cross-Eyes, posing as a doctor, selling charms against sickness, giving good hunting, exchanging promises of fair weather for good meat and skins, sending the death-stick, performing a thousand abominations. Yet I say to you, that when he says he can do these things, he lies. I, Professor Smith, Professor James Howard Smith, say that he lies. I have told him so to his teeth. Why has he not sent me the death-stick? Because he knows that with me it is without avail. But you, Hare-Lip, so deeply are you sunk in black superstition that did you awake this night and find the death-stick beside you, you would surely die. And you would die, not becaue of any virtues in the stick, but because you are a savage with the dark and clouded mind of a savage.

'The doctors must be destroyed, and all that was lost must be discovered over again. Wherefore, earnestly, I repeat unto you certain things which you must remember and tell to your children after you. You must tell them that when water is made hot by fire, there resides in it a wonderful thing called steam, which is stronger than ten thousand men and which can do all man's work for him. There are other very useful things. In the lightning flash resides a similarly strong servant of man, which was of old his slave and which some day will be his slave again.

'Quite a different thing is the alphabet. It is what enables me to know the meaning of fine markings, whereas you boys know only rude picture-writing. In that dry cave on Telegraph Hill, where you see me often go when the tribe is down by the sea, I have stored many books. In them is great wisdom. Also, with them, I have placed a key to the alphabet, so that one who knows picture-writing may also know print. Some day men will read again; and then, if no accident has befallen my cave, they will know that Professor James Howard Smith once lived and saved for them the knowledge of the ancients.

'There is another little device that men inevitably will rediscover. It is called gunpowder. It was what enabled us to kill surely and at long distances. Certain things which are found in the ground, when combined in the right proportions, will make this gunpowder. What these things are, I have forgotten, or else I never knew. But I wish I did know. Then would I make powder, and then would I certainly kill Cross-Eyes and rid the land of superstition——'

'After I am man-grown I am going to give Cross-Eyes all the goats, and meat, and skins I can get, so that he'll teach me to be a doctor,' Hoo-Hoo asserted. 'And when I know, I'll make everybody else sit up and take notice. They'll get down in the dirt to me, you bet.'

The old man nodded his head solemnly, and murmured:

'Strange it is to hear the vestiges and remnants of the complicated Aryan speech falling from the lips of a filthy little skin-clad savage. All the world is topsy-turvy. And it has been topsy-turvy ever since the plague.'

'You won't make me sit up,' Hare-Lip boasted to the would-be medicine-man. 'If I paid you for a sending of the death-stick and it didn't work, I'd bust in your head – understand, you Hoo-Hoo, you?'

'I'm going to get Granser to remember this here gunpowder stuff,' Edwin said softly, 'and then I'll have you all on the run. You, Hare-Lip, will do my fighting for me and get my meat for me and you, Hoo-Hoo, will send the death-stick for me and make everybody afraid. And if I catch Hare-Lip trying to bust your head, Hoo-Hoo, I'll fix him with that same gunpowder. Granser ain't such a fool as you think, and I'm going to listen to him and some day I'll be boss over the whole bunch of you.'

The old man shook his head sadly, and said:

'The gunpowder will come. Nothing can stop it – the same old story over and over. Man will increase, and men will fight. The gunpowder will enable men to kill millions of men, and in this way only, by fire and blood, will a new civilization, in some remote day, be evolved. And of what profit will it be? Just as the old civilization passed, so will the new. It may take fifty thousand years to build, but it will pass. All things pass. Only remains cosmic force and matter, ever in flux, ever acting and reacting and realizing the eternal types – the priest, the soldier, and the king. Out of the mouths of babes comes the wisdom of all the ages. Some will fight, some will rule, some will pray; and all the rest will toil and suffer sore while on their bleeding carcasses is reared again, and yet again, without end, the amazing beauty and surpassing wonder of the civilized state. It were just as well that I destroyed those cave-stored books – whether they remain or perish, all their old truths will be discovered, their old lies lived and handed down. What is the profit——'

Hare-Lip leaped to his feet, giving a quick glance at the pasturing goats and the afternoon sun.

'Gee!' he muttered to Edwin. 'The old geezer gets more long-winded every day. Let's pull for camp.'

While the other two, aided by the dogs, assembled the goats and started them for the trail through the forest, Edwin stayed by the old man and guided him in the same direction. When they reached the old right-of-way, Edwin stopped suddenly and looked back. Hare-Lip and Hoo-Hoo and the dogs and the goats passed on. Edwin was looking at a small herd of wild horses which had come down on the hard sand. There were at least twenty of them, young colts and yearlings and mares, led by a beautiful stallion which stood in the foam at the edge of the surf, with arched neck and bright wild eyes, sniffing the salt air from off the sea.

'What is it?' Granser queried.

'Horses,' was the answer. 'First time I ever seen 'em on the beach. It's the mountain lions getting thicker and thicker and driving 'em down.'

The low sun shot red shafts of light, fan-shaped, up from a cloud-tumbled horizon. And close at hand, in the white waste of shore-lashed waters, the sea-lions, bellowing their old primeval chant, hauled up out of the sea on the black rocks and fought and loved.

'Come on, Granser,' Edwin prompted.

And old man and boy, skin-clad and barbaric, turned and went along the right-of-way into the forest in the wake of the goats.

THE DREAM OF DEBS

I awoke fully an hour before my customary time. This in itself was remarkable, and I lay very wide awake, pondering over it. Something was the matter, something was wrong – I knew not what. I was oppressed by a premonition of something terrible that had happened or was about to happen. But what was it? I strove to orient myself. I remembered that at the time of the Great Earthquake of 1906 many claimed that they awakened some moments before the first shock and that during these moments they experienced strange feelings of dread. Was San Francisco again to be visited by earthquake?

I lay there for a full minute, numbly expectant, but there occurred no reeling of walls nor shock and grind of falling masonry. All was quiet. That was it! The silence! No wonder I had been perturbed. The hum of the great live city was strangely absent. The surface cars passed along my street, at that time of day, on an average of one every three minutes; but in the ten succeeding minutes not a car passed. Perhaps it was a street-railway strike, was my thought; or perhaps there had been an accident and the power was shut off. But no, the silence was too profound. I heard no jar and rattle of wagon wheels, nor stamp of iron-shod hoofs straining up the steep cobble-stones.

Pressing the push-button beside my bed, I strove to hear the sound of the bell, though I well knew it was impossible for the sound to rise three stories to me even if the bell did ring. It rang all right, for a few minutes later Brown entered with the tray and morning paper. Though his features were impassive as ever, I noted a startled, apprehensive light in his eyes. I noted, also, that there was no cream on the tray.

'The creamery did not deliver this morning,' he explained; 'nor did the bakery.'

I glanced again at the tray. There were no fresh French rolls – only slices of stale graham bread from yesterday, the most detestable of bread so far as I was concerned.

'Nothing was delivered this morning, sir,' Brown started to explain apologetically; but I interrupted him.

'The paper?'

'Yes, sir, it was delivered, but it was the only thing, and it is the last time, too. There won't be any paper tomorrow. The paper says so. Can I send out and get you some condensed milk?'

41

I shook my head, accepted the coffee black, and spread open the paper. The headlines explained everything – explained too much, in fact, for the lengths of pessimism to which the journal went were ridiculous. A general strike, it said, had been called all over the United States; and most foreboding anxieties were expressed concerning the provisioning of the great cities.

I read on hastily, skimming much and remembering much of labour troubles in the past. For a generation the general strike had been the dream of organized labour, which dream had arisen originally in the mind of Debs, one of the great labour leaders of thirty years before. I recollected that in my young college-settlement days I had even written an article on the subject for one of the magazines and that I had entitled it 'The Dream of Debs'. And I must confess that I had treated the idea very cavalierly and academically as a dream and nothing more. Time and the world had rolled on, Gompers was gone, the American Federation of Labour was gone, and gone was Debs with all his wild revolutionary ideas; but the dream had persisted, and here it was at last realized in fact. But I laughed, as I read, at the journal's gloomy outlook. I knew better. I had seen organized labour worsted in too many conflicts. It would be a matter only of days when the thing would be settled. This was a national strike, and it wouldn't take the Government long to break it.

I threw the paper down and proceeded to dress. It would certainly be interesting to be out in the streets of San Francisco when not a wheel was turning and the whole city was taking an enforced vacation.

'I beg your pardon, sir,' Brown said, as he handed me my cigar-case, 'but Mr Harmmed has asked to see you before you go out.'

'Send him in right away,' I answered.

Harmmed was the butler. When he entered I could see he was labouring under controlled excitement. He came at once to the point.

'What shall I do, sir? There will be needed provisions, and the delivery drivers are on strike. And the electricity is shut off – I guess they're on strike, too.'

'Are the shops open?' I asked.

'Only the small ones, sir. The retail clerks are out, and the big ones can't open; but the owners and their families are running the little ones themselves.'

'Then take the machine,' I said, 'and go the rounds and make your purchases. Buy plenty of everything you need or may need. Get a box of candles – no, get half-a-dozen boxes. And, when you're done, tell Harrison to bring the machine around to the club for me – not later than eleven.'

Harmmed shook his head gravely. 'Mr Harrison has struck along with the Chauffeurs' Union, and I don't know how to run the machine myself.'

'Oh, ho, he has, has he?' I said. 'Well, when next *Mister* Harrison happens around you tell him that he can look elsewhere for a position.'

'Yes, sir.'

'You don't happen to belong to a Butlers' Union, do you, Harmmed?'

'No, sir,' was the answer. 'And even if I did I'd not desert my employer in a crisis like this. No, sir, I would——'

'All right, thank you,' I said. 'Now you get ready to accompany me. I'll run the machine myself, and we'll lay in a stock of provisions to stand a siege.'

It was a beautiful first of May, even as May days go. The sky was cloudless, there was no wind, and the air was warm – almost balmy. Many autos were out, but the owners were driving them themselves. The streets were crowded but quiet. The working class, dressed in its Sunday best, was out taking the air and observing the effects of the strike. It was all so unusual, and withal so peaceful, that I found myself enjoying it. My nerves were tingling with mild excitement. It was a sort of placid adventure. I passed Miss Chickering. She was at the helm of her little runabout. She swung around and came after me, catching me at the corner.

'Oh, Mr Corf!' she hailed. 'Do you know where I can buy candles? I've been to a dozen shops, and they're all sold out. It's dreadfully awful, isn't it?'

But her sparkling eyes gave the lie to her words. Like the rest of us, she was enjoying it hugely. Quite an adventure it was, getting those candles. It was not until we went across the city and down into the working-class quarter south of Market Street that we found small corner groceries that had not yet sold out. Miss Chickering thought one box was sufficient, but I persuaded her into taking four. My car was large, and I laid in a dozen boxes. There was no telling what delays might arise in the settlement of the strike. Also, I filled the car with sacks of flour, baking-powder, tinned goods, and all the ordinary necessities of life suggested by Harmmed, who fussed around and clucked over the purchases like an anxious old hen.

The remarkable thing, that first day of the strike, was that no one really apprehended anything serious. The announcement of organized labour in the morning papers that it was prepared to stay out a month or three months was laughed at. And yet that very first day we might have guessed as much from the fact that the working class took practically no part in the great rush to buy provisions. Of course not. For weeks and months, craftily and secretly, the whole working class had been laying in private stocks of provisions. That was why we were permitted to go down and buy out the little groceries in the working-class neighbourhoods.

It was not until I arrived at the club that afternoon that I began to feel the first alarm. Everything was in confusion. There were no olives for the cocktails, and the service was by hitches and jerks. Most of the men were angry, and all were worried. A babel of voices greeted me as I entered. General Folsom, nursing his capacious paunch in a window-seat in the smoking-room, was defending himself against half-a-dozen excited gentlemen who were demanding that he should do something.

'What can I do more than I have done?' he was saying. 'There are no orders from Washington. If you gentlemen will get a wire through I'll do anything I am commanded to do. But I don't see what can be done. The first thing I did this morning, as soon as I learned of the strike, was to order in the troops from the Presidio – three thousand of them. They're guarding the banks, the Mint, the post office, and all the public buildings. There is no disorder whatever. The strikers are keeping the peace perfectly. You can't expect me to shoot them down as they walk along the streets with wives and children all in their best bib and tucker.'

'I'd like to know what's happening on Wall Street,' I heard Jimmy Wombold say as I passed along. I could imagine his anxiety, for I knew that he was deep in the big Consolidated-Western deal.

'Say, Corf,' Atkinson bustled up to me, 'is your machine running?'

'Yes,' I answered, 'but what's the matter with your own?'

'Broken down, and the garages are all closed. And my wife's somewhere around Truckee, I think, stalled on the overland. Can't get a wire to her for love or money. She should have arrived this evening. She may be starving. Lend me your machine.'

'Can't get it across the bay,' Halstead spoke up. 'The ferries aren't running. But I tell you what you can do. There's Rollinson – oh, Rollinson, come here a moment. Atkinson wants to get a machine across the bay. His wife is stuck on the overland at Truckee. Can't you bring the *Lurlette* across from Tiburon and carry the machine over for him?'

The *Lurlette* was a two-hundred-ton, ocean-going schooner-yacht.

Rollinson shook his head. 'You couldn't get a longshoreman to land the machine on board, even if I could get the *Lurlette* over, which I can't, for the crew are members of the Coast Seamen's union, and they're on strike along with the rest.'

'But my wife may be starving,' I could hear Atkinson wailing as I moved on.

At the other end of the smoking-room I ran into a group of men bunched excitedly and angrily around Bertie Messener. And Bertie was stirring them up and prodding them in his cool, cynical way. Bertie didn't care about the strike. He didn't care much about anything. He was blasé – at least in all the clean things of life; the nasty things had no attraction for him. He was worth twenty millions, all of it in safe investments, and he had never done a tap of productive work in his life –

inherited it all from his father and two uncles. He had been everywhere, seen everything, and done everything except get married, and this last in the face of the grim and determined attack of a few hundred ambitious mammas. For years he had been the greatest catch, and as yet he had avoided being caught. He was disgracefully eligible. On top of his wealth he was young, handsome, and, as I said before, clean. He was a great athlete, a young blond god that did everything perfectly and admirably with the solitary exception of matrimony. And he didn't care about anything, had no ambitions, no passions, no desire to do the very things he did so much better than other men.

'This is sedition!' one man in the group was crying. Another called it revolt and revolution, and another called it anarchy.

'I can't see it,' Bertie said. 'I have been out in the streets all morning. Perfect order reigns. I never saw a more law-abiding populace. There's no use calling it names. It's not any of those things. It's just what it claims to be, a general strike, and it's your turn to play, gentlemen.'

'And we'll play all right!' cried Garfield, one of the traction millionaires. 'We'll show this dirt where its place is – the beasts! Wait till the Government takes a hand.'

'But where is the Government?' Bertie interposed. 'It might as well be at the bottom of the sea so far as you're concerned. You don't know what's happening at Washington. You don't know whether you've got a Government or not.'

'Don't you worry about that,' Garfield blurted out.

'I assure you I'm not worrying,' Bertie smiled languidly. 'But it seems to me it's what you fellows are doing. Look in the glass, Garfield.'

Garfield did not look, but had he looked he would have seen a very excited gentleman with rumpled, iron-grey hair, a flushed face, mouth sullen and vindictive, and eyes wildly gleaming.

'It's not right, I tell you,' little Hanover said; and from his tone I was sure that he had already said it a number of times.

'Now that's going too far, Hanover,' Bertie replied. 'You fellows make me tired. You're all open-shop men. You've eroded my eardrums with your endless gabble for the open shop and the right of a man to work. You've harangued along those lines for years. Labour is doing nothing wrong in going out on this general strike. It is violating no law of God nor man. Don't you talk, Hanover. You've been ringing the changes too long on the God-given right to work . . . or not to work; you can't escape the corollary. It's a dirty little sordid scrap, that's all the whole thing is. You've got labour down and gouged it, and now labour's got you down and is gouging you, that's all, and you're squealing.'

Every man in the group broke out in indignant denials that labour had ever been gouged.

'No, sir!' Garfield was shouting. 'We've done the best for labour. Instead of gouging it, we've given it a chance to live. We've made work for it. Where would labour be if it hadn't been for us?'

'A whole lot better off,' Bertie sneered. 'You've got labour down and gouged it every time you got a chance and you went out of your way to make chances.'

'No! No!' were the cries.

'There was the teamsters' strike, right here in San Francisco,' Bertie went on imperturbably. 'The Employers' Association precipitated that strike. You know that. And you know I know it, too, for I've sat in these very rooms and heard the inside talk and news of the fight. First you precipitated the strike, then you bought the Mayor and the Chief of Police and broke the strike. A pretty spectacle, you philanthropists getting the teamsters down and gouging them.

'Hold on, I'm not through with you. It's only last year that the labour ticket of Colorado elected a governor. He was never seated. You know why. You know how your brother philanthropists and capitalists of Colorado worked it. It was a case of getting labour down and gouging it. You kept the president of the South-western Amalgamated Association of Miners in jail for three years on trumped-up murder charges, and with him out of the way you broke up the association. That was gouging labour, you'll admit. The third time the graduated income tax was declared unconstitutional was a gouge. So was the eight-hour Bill you killed in the last Congress.

'And of all unmitigated immoral gouges, your destruction of the closed-shop principle was the limit. You know how it was done. You bought out Farburg, the last president of the old American Federation of Labour. He was your creature – or the creature of all the trusts and employers' associations, which is the same thing. You precipitated the big closed-shop strike. Farburg betrayed that strike. You won, and the old American Federation of Labour crumbled to pieces. You fellows destroyed it, and by so doing undid yourselves; for right on top of it began the organization of the I.L.W. – the biggest and solidest organization of labour the United States has ever seen, and you are responsible for its existence and for the present general strike. You smashed all the old federations and drove labour into the I.L.W., and the I.L.W. called the general strike – still fighting for the closed shop. And then you have the effrontery to stand here face to face and tell me that you never got labour down and gouged it. Bah!'

This time there were no denials. Garfield broke out in self-defence –

'We've done nothing we were not compelled to do, if we were to win.'

'I'm not saying anything about that,' Bertie answered. 'What I am complaining about is your squealing now that you're getting a taste of your own medicine. How many strikes have you won by starving labour into submission? Well, labour's worked out a scheme whereby to starve you into submission. It wants the closed shop, and, if it can get it by starving you, why, starve you shall.'

'I notice that you have profited in the past by those very labour gouges you mention,' insinuated Brentwood, one of the wiliest and most astute of our corporation lawyers. 'The receiver is as bad as the thief,' he sneered. 'You had no hand in the gouging, but you took your whack out of the gouge.'

'That is quite beside the question, Brentwood,' Bertie drawled. 'You're as bad as Hanover, intruding the moral element. I haven't said that anything is right or wrong. It's all a rotten game, I know; and my sole kick is that you fellows are squealing now that you're down and labour's taking a gouge out of you. Of course I've taken the profits from the gouging and, thanks to you, gentlemen, without having personally to do the dirty work. You did that for me – oh, believe me, not because I am more virtuous than you, but because my good father and his various brothers left me a lot of money with which to pay for the dirty work.'

'If you mean to insinuate——' Brentwood began hotly.

'Hold on, don't get all – ruffled up,' Bertie interposed insolently. 'There's no use in playing hypocrites in this thieves' den. The high and lofty is all right for the newspapers, boys' clubs, and Sunday schools – that's part of the game; but for heaven's sake don't let's play it on one another. You know, and you know that I know, just what jobbery was done in the building trades' strike last fall, who put up the money, who did the work, and who profited by it.' (Brentwood flushed darkly.) 'But we are all tarred with the same brush, and the best thing for us to do is to leave morality out of it. Again I repeat, play the game, play it to the last finish, but for goodness' sake don't squeal when you get hurt.'

When I left the group Bertie was off on a new tack tormenting them with the more serious aspect of the situation, pointing out the shortage of supplies that was already making itself felt, and asking them what they were going to do about it. A little later I met him in the cloak-room, leaving, and gave him a lift home in my machine.

'It's a great stroke, this general strike,' he said, as we bowled along through the crowded but orderly streets. 'It's a smashing body-blow. Labour caught us napping and struck at our weakest place, the stomach. I'm going to get out of San Francisco, Corf. Take my advice and get out, too. Head for the country, anywhere. You'll have more chance. Buy up a stock of supplies and get into a tent or a cabin somewhere. Soon there'll be nothing but starvation in this city for such as we.'

How correct Bertie Messener was I never dreamed. I decided that he was an alarmist. As for myself, I was content to remain and watch the fun. After I dropped him, instead of going directly home, I went on in a hunt for more food. To my surprise, I learned that the small groceries where I had bought in the morning were sold out. I extended my search to the Potrero, and by good luck managed to pick up another box of candles, two sacks of wheat flour, ten pounds of graham flour (which would do for the servants), a case of tinned corn, and two cases of tinned tomatoes. It did look as though there was going to be at least a temporary food shortage, and I hugged myself over the goodly stock of provisions I had laid in.

The next morning I had my coffee in bed as usual, and, more than the cream, I missed the daily paper. It was this absence of knowledge of what was going on in the world that I found the chief hardship. Down at the club there was little news. Rider had crossed from Oakland in his launch, and Halstead had been down to San Jose and back in his machine. They reported the same conditions in those places as in San Francisco. Everything was tied up by the strike. All grocery stocks had been bought out by the upper classes. And perfect order reigned. But what was happening over the rest of the country – in Chicago? New York? Washington? Most probably the same things that were happening with us, we concluded; but the fact that we did not know with absolute surety was irritating.

General Folsom had a bit of news. An attempt had been made to place army telegraphers in the telegraph offices, but the wires had been cut in every direction. This was, so far, the one unlawful act committed by labour, and that it was a concerted act he was fully convinced. He had communicated by wireless with the army post at Benicia, the telegraph lines were even then being patrolled by soldiers all the way to Sacramento. Once, for one short instant, they had got the Sacramento call, then the wires, somewhere, were cut again. General Folsom reasoned that similar attempts to open communication were being made by the authorities all the way across the continent, but he was non-committal as to whether or not he thought the attempt would succeed. What worried him was the wire-cutting; he could not but believe that it was an important part of the deep-laid labour conspiracy. Also, he regretted that the Government had not long since established its projected chain of wireless stations.

The days came and went, and for a while it was a hum-drum time. Nothing happened. The edge of excitement had become blunted. The streets were not so crowded. The working class did not come uptown any more to see how we were taking the strike. And there were not so many automobiles running around. The repair-shops and garages were closed, and whenever a machine broke down it went out of commission. The clutch on mine broke, and neither love nor money could get it repaired. Like the rest, I was now walking. San Francisco lay dead, and we did not know what was happening over the rest of the country. But from the very fact that we did not know we could conclude only that the rest of the country lay as dead as San Francisco. From time to time the city was placarded with the proclamations of organized labour – these had been printed months before, and evidenced how thoroughly the I.L.W. had prepared for the strike. Every detail had been worked out long in advance. No violence had occurred as yet, with the exception of the shooting of a few wire-cutters by the soldiers, but the people of the slums were starving and growing ominously restless.

The business men, the millionaires, and the professional class held meetings and passed resolutions, but there was no way of making the proclamations public. They could not even get them printed. One result of these meetings, however, was that General Folsom was persuaded into taking military possession of the wholesale houses and of all the flour, grain, and food warehouses. It was high time, for suffering was becoming acute in the homes of the rich, and breadlines were necessary. I knew that my servants were beginning to draw long faces, and it was amazing – the hole they made in my stock of provisions. In fact, as I afterwards surmised, each servant was stealing from me and secreting a private stock of provisions for himself.

But with the formation of the bread-lines came new troubles. There was only so much of a food reserve in San Francisco, and at the best it could not last long. Organized labour, we knew, had its private supplies; nevertheless, the whole working class joined the bread-lines. As a result, the provisions General Folsom had taken possession of diminished with perilous rapidity. How were the soldiers to distinguish between a shabby middle-class man, a member of the I.L.W., or a slum dweller? The first and the last had to be fed, but the soldiers did not know all the I.L.W. men in the city, much less the wives and sons and daughters of the I.L.W. men. The employers helping, a few of the known union men were flung out of the bread-lines; but that amounted to nothing. To make matters worse, the Government tugs that had been hauling food from the army depots on Mare Island to Angel Island found no more food to haul. The soldiers now received their rations from the confiscated provisions, and they received them first.

The beginning of the end was in sight. Violence was beginning to show its face. Law and order were passing away, and passing away, I must confess, among the slum people and the upper classes. Organized labour still maintained perfect order. It could well afford to – it had plenty to eat. I remember the afternoon at the club when I caught Halstead and Brentwood whispering in a corner. They took me in on the venture. Brentwood's machine was still in running order, and they were going out cow-stealing. Halstead had a long butcher knife and a cleaver. We went out to the outskirts of the city. Here and there were cows grazing, but always they were guarded by their owners. We pursued our quest, following along the fringe of the city to the east, and on the hills near Hunter's Point we came upon a cow guarded by a little girl. There was also a young calf with the cow. We wasted no time on preliminaries. The little girl ran away screaming, while we slaughtered the cow. I omit the details, for they are not nice – we were unaccustomed to such work, and we bungled it.

But in the midst of it, working with the haste of fear, we heard cries, and we saw a number of men running towards us. We abandoned the spoils and took to our heels. To our surprise we were not pursued. Looking back, we saw the men hurriedly cutting up the cow. They had been on the same lay as ourselves. We argued that there was plenty for all, and ran back. The scene that followed beggars description. We fought and squabbled over the division like savages. Brentwood, I remember, was a perfect brute, snarling and snapping and threatening that murder would be done if we did not get our proper share.

And we were getting our share when there occurred a new irruption on the scene. This time it was the dreaded peace officers of the I.L.W. The little girl had brought them. They were armed with whips and clubs, and there were a score of them. The little girl danced up and down in anger, the tears streaming down her cheeks, crying: 'Give it to 'em! Give it to 'em! That guy with the specs – he did it! Mash his face for him! Mash his face!' That guy with the specs was I, and I got my face mashed, too, though I had the presence of mind to take off my glasses at the first. My! but we did receive a trouncing as we scattered in all directions. Brentwood, Halstead and I fled away for the machine. Brentwood's nose was bleeding, while Halstead's cheek was cut across with the scarlet slash of a black-snake whip.

And lo, when the pursuit ceased and we had gained the machine, there, hiding behind it, was the frightened calf. Brentwood warned us to be cautious, and crept up on it like a wolf or a tiger. Knife and cleaver had been left behind, but Brentwood still had his hands, and over and over on the ground he rolled with the poor little calf as he throttled it. We threw the carcass into the machine, covered it over with a robe, and started for home. But our misfortunes had only begun. We blew out a tyre. There was no way of fixing it, and twilight was coming on. We abandoned the machine, Brentwood puffing and staggering along in advance, the calf, covered by the robe, slung across his shoulders. We took turn about carrying that calf, and it nearly killed us. Also, we lost our way. And then, after hours of wandering and toil, we encountered a gang of hoodlums. They were not I.L.W. men, and I guess they were as hungry as we. At any rate, they got the calf and we got the thrashing. Brentwood raged like a madman the rest of the way home, and he looked like one, with his torn clothes, swollen nose, and blackened eyes.

There wasn't any more cow-stealing after that. General Folsom sent his troopers out and confiscated all the cows, and his troopers, aided by the militia, ate most of the meat. General Folsom was not to be blamed; it was his duty to maintain law and order, and he maintained it by means of the soldiers, wherefore he was compelled to feed them first of all.

It was about this time that the great panic occurred. The wealthy classes precipitated the flight, and then the slum people caught the contagion and stampeded wildly out of the city. General Folsom was pleased. It was estimated that at least 200,000 had deserted San Francisco, and by that much was his food problem solved. Well do I remember that day. In the morning I had eaten a crust of bread. Half the afternoon I had stood in the bread-line; and after dark I returned home, tired and miserable, carrying a quart of rice and a slice of bacon. Brown met me at the door. His face was worn and terrified. All the servants had fled, he informed me. He alone remained. I was touched by his faithfulness and, when I learned that he had eaten nothing all day, I divided my food with him. We cooked half the rice and half the bacon, sharing it equally and reserving the other half for morning. I went to bed with my hunger, and tossed restlessly all night. In the morning I found Brown had deserted me, and, greater misfortune still, he had stolen what remained of the rice and bacon.

It was a gloomy handful of men that came together at the club that morning. There was no service at all. The last servant was gone. I noticed, too, that the silver was gone, and I learned where it had gone. The servants had not taken it, for the reason, I presume, that the club members got to it first. Their method of disposing of it was simple. Down south of Market Street, in the dwellings of the I.L.W., the housewives had given square meals in exchange for it. I went back to my house. Yes, my silver was gone — all but a massive pitcher. This I wrapped up and carried down south of Market Street.

I felt better after the meal, and returned to the club to learn if there was anything new in the situation. Hanover, Collins and Dakon were just leaving. There was no one inside, they told me, and they invited me to come along with them. They were leaving the city, they said, on Dakon's horses, and there was a spare one for me. Dakon had four magnificent carriage horses that he wanted to save, and General Folsom had given him the tip that next morning all the horses that remained in the city were to be confiscated for food. There were not many horses left, for tens of thousands of them had been turned loose into the country when the hay and grain gave out during the first days. Birdall, I remember, who had great draying interests, had turned loose three hundred dray horses. At an average value of five hundred dollars, this had amounted to $150,000. He had hoped at first to recover most of the horses after the strike was over, but in the end he never recovered one of them. They were all eaten by the people that fled from San Francisco. For that matter, the killing of the army mules and horses for food had already begun.

Fortunately for Dakon, he had had a plentiful supply of hay and grain stored in his stable. We managed to raise four saddles, and we found the animals in good condition and spirited, withal unused to being ridden. I remembered the San Francisco of the great earthquake as we rode through the streets, but this San Francisco was vastly more pitiable. No cataclysm of nature had caused this, but, rather, the tyranny of the labour unions. We rode down past Union Square and through the theatre, hotel, and shopping districts. The streets were deserted. Here and there stood automobiles, abandoned where they had broken down or when the gasoline had given out. There was no sign of life, save for the occasional policeman and the soldiers guarding the banks and public buildings. Once we came upon an I.L.W. man pasting up the latest proclamation. We stopped to read. 'We have maintained an orderly strike,' it ran; 'and we shall maintain order to the end. The end will come when our demands are satisfied, and our demands will be satisfied when we have starved our employers into submission, as we ourselves in the past have often been starved into submission.'

'Messener's very words,' Collins said. 'And I, for one, am ready to submit, only they won't give me a chance to submit. I haven't had a full meal in an age. I wonder what horse-meat tastes like?'

We stopped to read another proclamation: 'When we think our employers are ready to submit we shall open up the telegraphs and place the employers' associations of the United States in communication. But only messages relating to peace terms shall be permitted over the wires.'

We rode on, crossed Market Street, and a little later were passing through the working-class district. Here the streets were not deserted. Leaning over the gates or standing in groups were the I.L.W. men. Happy, well-fed children were playing games, and stout housewives sat on the front steps gossiping. One and all cast amused glances at us. Little children ran after us, crying: 'Hey, mister, ain't you hungry?' And one woman, nursing a child at her breast, called to Dakon: 'Say, Fatty, I'll give you a meal for your skate – ham and potatoes, currant jelly, white bread, canned butter, and two cups of coffee.'

'Have you noticed, the last few days,' Hanover remarked to me, 'that there's not been a stray dog in the streets?'

I had noticed, but I had not thought about it before. It was high time to leave the unfortunate city. We at last managed to connect with the San

Bruno Road, along which we headed south. I had a country place near Menlo, and it was our objective. But soon we began to discover that the country was worse off and far more dangerous than the city. There the soldiers and the I.L.W. kept order; but the country had been turned over to anarchy. Two hundred thousand people had fled from San Francisco, and we had countless evidences that their flight had been like that of an army of locusts.

They had swept everything clean. There had been robbery and fighting. Here and there we passed bodies by the roadside and saw the blackened ruins of farm-houses. The fences were down, and the crops had been trampled by the feet of a multitude. All the vegetable patches had been rooted up by the famished hordes. All the chickens and farm animals had been slaughtered. This was true of all the main roads that led out of San Francisco. Here and there, away from the roads, farmers had held their own with shotguns and revolvers, and were still holding their own. They warned us away and refused to parley with us. And all the destruction and violence had been done by the slum-dwellers and the upper classes. The I.L.W. men, with plentiful food supplies, remained quietly in their homes in the cities.

Early in the ride we received concrete proof of how desperate was the situation. To the right of us we heard cries and rifle-shots. Bullets whistled dangerously near. There was a crashing in the underbush; then a magnificent black truck-horse broke across the road in front of us and was gone. We had barely time to notice that he was bleeding and lame. He was followed by three soldiers. The chase went on among the trees on the left. We could hear the soldiers calling to one another. A fourth soldier limped out upon the road from the right, sat down on a boulder, and mopped the sweat from his face.

'Militia,' Dakon whispered. 'Deserters.'

The man grinned up at us and asked for a match. In reply to Dakon's 'What's the word?' he informed us that the militiamen were deserting. 'No grub,' he explained. 'They're feedin' it all to the regulars.' We also learned from him that the military prisoners had been released from Alcatraz Island because they could no longer be fed.

I shall never forget the next sight we encountered. We came upon it abruptly around a turn of the road. Overhead arched the trees. The sunshine was filtering down through the branches. Butterflies were fluttering by, and from the fields came the song of the larks. And there it stood, a powerful touring car. About it and in it lay a number of corpses. It told its own tale. Its occupants, fleeing from the city, had been attacked and dragged down by a gang of slum dwellers – hoodlums. The thing had occurred within twenty-four hours. Freshly opened meat and fruit tins explained the reason for the attack. Dakon examined the bodies.

'I thought so,' he reported. 'I've ridden in that car. It was Perriton – the whole family. We've got to watch out for ourselves from now on.'

'But we have no food with which to invite attack,' I objected.

Dakon pointed to the horse I rode, and I understood.

Early in the day Dakon's horse had cast a shoe. The delicate hoof had split, and by noon the animal was limping. Dakon refused to ride it further, and refused to desert it. So, on his solicitation, we went on. He would lead the horse and join us at my place. That was the last we saw of him; nor did we ever learn his end.

By one o'clock we arrived at the town of Menlo, or, rather, at the site of Menlo, for it was in ruins. Corpses lay everywhere. The business part of the town, as well as part of the residences, had been gutted by fire. Here and there a residence still held out; but there was no getting near them. When we approached too closely we were fired upon. We met a woman who was poking about in the smoking ruins of her cottage. The first attack, she told us, had been on the stores, and as she talked we could picture that raging, roaring, hungry mob flinging itself on the handful of townspeople. Millionaires and paupers had fought side by side for the food, and then fought with one another after they got it. The town of Pao Alto and Stanford University had been sacked in similar fashion, we learned. Ahead of us lay a desolate, wasted land; and we thought we were wise in turning off to my place. It lay three miles to the west, snuggling among the first rolling swells of the foothills.

But as we rode along we saw that the devastation was not confined to the main roads. The van of the flight had kept to the roads, sacking the small towns as it went; while those that followed had scattered out and swept the whole countryside like a great broom. My place was built of concrete, masonry and tiles, and so had escaped being burned, but it was gutted clean. We found the gardener's body in the windmill, littered around with empty shot-gun shells. He had put up a good fight. But no trace could we find of the two Italian labourers, nor of the housekeeper and her husband. Not a live thing remained. The calves, the colts, all the fancy poultry and thoroughbred stock, everything was gone. The kitchen and the fireplaces, where the mob had cooked, were a mess, while many campfires outside bore witness to the large number that had fed and spent the night. What they had not eaten they had carried away. There was not a bite for us.

We spent the rest of the night vainly waiting for Dakon, and in the morning, with our revolvers, fought off half-a-dozen marauders. Then we killed one of Dakon's horses, hiding for the future what meat we did not immediately eat. In the afternoon Collins went out for a walk, but failed to return. This was the last straw to Hanover. He was for flight there and then, and I had great difficulty in persuading him to wait for daylight. As for myself, I was convinced that the end of the general strike was near, and I was resolved to return to San Francisco. So, in the morning, we parted company, Hanover heading south, fifty pounds of horsemeat strapped to his saddle, while I, similarly loaded, headed north. Little Hanover pulled through all right, and to the end of his life he will persist, I know, in boring everybody with the narrative of his subsequent adventures.

I got as far as Belmont, on the main road back, when I was robbed of my horse-meat by three militiamen. There was no change in the situation, they said, except that it was going from bad to worse. The I.L.W. had plenty of provisions hidden away and could last out for months. I managed to get as far as Baden, when my horse was taken away from me by a dozen men. Two of them were San Francisco policemen, and the remainder were regular soldiers. This was ominous. The situation was certainly extreme when the regulars were beginning to desert. When I continued my way on foot, they already had the fire started, and the last of Dakon's horses lay slaughtered on the ground.

As luck would have it, I sprained my ankle, and succeeded in getting no farther than South San Francisco. I lay there that night in an outhouse, shivering with the cold and at the same time burning with fever. Two days I lay there, too sick to move, and on the third, reeling and giddy, supporting myself on an extemporized crutch, I tottered on towards San Francisco. I was weak as well, for it was the third day since food had passed my lips. It was a day of nightmare and torment. As in a dream I passed hundreds of regular soldiers drifting along in the opposite direction, and many policemen, with their families, organized in large groups for mutual protection.

As I entered the city I remembered the workman's house at which I had traded the silver pitcher, and in that direction my hunger drove me. Twilight was falling when I came to the place. I passed around by the alleyway and crawled up the back steps, on which I collapsed. I managed to reach out with the crutch and knock on the door. Then I must have fainted, for I came to in the kitchen, my face wet with water, and whisky being poured down my throat. I choked and spluttered and tried to talk. I began saying something about not having any more silver pitchers, but that I would make it up to them afterwards if they would only give me something to eat. But the housewife interrupted me.

'Why, you poor man,' she said, 'haven't you heard? The strike was called off this afternoon. Of course we'll give you something to eat.'

She bustled around, opening a tin of breakfast bacon and preparing to fry it.

'Let me have some now, please,' I begged; and I ate the raw bacon on a slice of bread, while her husband explained that the demands of the

I.L.W. had been granted. The wires had been opened up in the early afternoon, and everywhere the employers' associations had given in. There hadn't been any employers left in San Francisco, but General Folsom had spoken for them. The trains and steamers would start running in the morning, and so would everything else just as soon as system could be established.

And that was the end of the general strike. I never want to see another one. It was worse than a war. A general strike is a cruel and immoral thing, and the brain of man should be capable of running industry in a more rational way. Harrison is still my chauffeur. It was part of the conditions of the I.L.W. that all of its members should be reinstated in their old positions. Brown never came back, but the rest of the servants are with me. I hadn't the heart to discharge them – poor creatures, they were pretty hard-pressed when they deserted with the food and silver. And now I can't discharge them. They have all been unionized by the I.L.W. The tyranny of organized labour is getting beyond endurance. Something must be done.

THE SHADOW AND THE FLASH

When I look back, I realize what a peculiar friendship it was. First, there was Lloyd Inwood, tall, slender, and finely knit, nervous and dark. And then Paul Tichlorne, tall, slender, and finely knit, nervous and blond. Each was the replica of the other in everything except colour. Lloyd's eyes were black; Paul's were blue. Under stress of excitement, the blood coursed olive in the face of Lloyd, crimson in the face of Paul. But outside this matter of colouring they were as like as two peas. Both were high-strung, prone to excessive tension and endurance, and they lived at concert pitch.

But there was a trio involved in this remarkable friendship, and the third was short, and fat, and chunky, and lazy, and, loath to say, it was I. Paul and Lloyd seemed born to rivalry with each other, and I to be peacemaker between them. We grew up together, the three of us, and full often have I received the angry blows each intended for the other. They were always competing, striving to outdo each other, and when entered upon some such struggle there was no limit to their endeavours or passions.

This intense spirit of rivalry obtained in their studies and their games. If Paul memorized one canto of 'Marmion', Lloyd memorized two cantos, Paul came back with three, and Lloyd again with four, till each knew the whole poem by heart. I remember an incident that occurred at the swimming hole – an incident tragically significant of the life-struggle between them. The boys had a game of diving to the bottom of a ten-foot pool and holding on by submerged roots to see who could stay under the longest. Paul and Lloyd allowed themselves to be bantered into making the descent together. When I saw their faces, set and determined, disappear in the water as they sank swiftly down, I felt a foreboding of something dreadful. The moments sped, the ripples died away, the face of the pool grew placid and untroubled, and neither black nor golden head broke surface in quest of air. We above grew anxious. The longest record of the longest-winded boy had been exceeded, and still there was no sign. Air bubbles trickled slowly upward, showing that the breath had been expelled from their lungs, and after that the bubbles ceased to trickle upward. Each second became interminable, and, unable longer to endure the suspense, I plunged into the water.

I found them down at the bottom, clutching tight to the roots, their heads not a foot apart, their eyes wide open, each glaring fixedly at the other. They were suffering frightful torment, writhing and twisting in the pangs of voluntary suffocation; for neither would let go and acknowledge himself beaten. I tried to break Paul's hold on the root, but he resisted me fiercely. Then I lost my breath and came to the surface, badly scared. I quickly explained the situation, and half a dozen of us went down and by main strength tore them loose. By the time we got them out, both were unconscious, and it was only after much barrel-rolling and rubbing and pounding that they finally came to their senses. They would have drowned there, had no one rescued them.

When Paul Tichlorne entered college, he let it be generally understood that he was going in for the social sciences. Lloyd Inwood, entering at the same time, elected to take the same course. But Paul had had it secretly in mind all the time to study the natural sciences, specializing on chemistry, and at the last moment he switched over. Though Lloyd had already arranged his year's work and attended the first lectures, he at once followed Paul's lead and went in for the natural sciences and especially for chemistry. Their rivalry soon became a noted thing throughout the university. Each was a spur to the other, and they went into chemistry deeper than ever students before – so deep, in fact, that ere they took their sheepskins they could have stumped any chemistry or 'cow college' professor in the institution, save 'old' Moss, head of the department, and even him they puzzled and edified more than once. Lloyd's discovery of the 'death bacillus' of the sea toad, and his experiments on it with potassium cyanide, sent his name and that of his university ringing round the world; nor was Paul a whit behind when he succeeded in producing laboratory colloids exhibiting amoeba-like activities, and when he cast new light upon the processes of fertilization through his startling experiments with simple sodium chloride and magnesium solutions on low forms of marine life.

It was in their undergraduate days, however, in the midst of their profoundest plunges into the mysteries of organic chemistry, that Doris Van Benschoten entered into their lives. Lloyd met her first, but within twenty-four hours Pahe also made her acquaintance. Of course, they fell in love with her, and she became the only thing in life worth living for. They wooed her with equal ardour and fire, and so intense became their struggle for her that half the student-body took to wagering wildly on the result. Even 'old' Moss, one day, after an astounding demonstration in his private laboratory by Paul, was guilty to the extent of a month's salary of backing him to become the bridegroom of Doris Van Benschoten.

In the end she solved the problem in her own way, to everybody's satisfaction except Paul's and Lloyd's. Getting them together, she said that she really could not choose between them because she loved them both equally well; and that, unfortunately, since polyandry was not permitted in the United States she would be compelled to forgo the honour and happiness of marrying either of them. Each blamed the other for this lamentable outcome, and the bitterness between them grew more bitter.

But things came to a head soon enough. It was at my home, after they had taken their degrees and dropped out of the world's sight, that the beginning of the end came to pass. Both were men of means, with little inclination and no necessity for professional life. My friendship and their mutual animosity were the two things that linked them in any way together. While they were very often at my place, they made it a fastidious point to avoid each other on such visits, though it was inevitable, under the circumstances, that they should come upon each other occasionally.

On the day I have in recollection, Paul Tichlorne had been mooning all morning in my study over a current scientific review. This left me free to my own affairs, and I was out among my roses when Lloyd Inwood arrived. Clipping and pruning and tacking the climbers on the porch, with my mouth full of nails, and Lloyd following me about and lending a hand now and again, we fell to discussing the mythical race of invisible people, that strange and vagrant people the traditions of which have come down to us. Lloyd warmed to the talk in his nervous, jerky fashion, and was soon interrogating the physical properties and possibilities of invisibility. A perfectly black object, he contended, would elude and defy the acutest vision.

'Colour is a sensation,' he was saying. 'It has no objective reality. Without light, we can see neither colours nor objects themselves. All objects are black in the dark, and in the dark it is impossible to see them. If no light strikes upon them, then no light is flung back from them to the eye, and so we have no vision-evidence of their being.'

'But we see black objects in daylight,' I objected.

'Very true,' he went on warmly. 'And that is because they are not perfectly black. Were they perfectly black, absolutely black, as it were, we could not see them – ay, not in the blaze of a thousand suns could we see them! And so I say, with the right pigments, properly compounded, an absolutely black paint could be produced which would render invisible whatever it was applied to.'

'It would be a remarkable discovery,' I said non-committally, for the whole thing seemed too fantastic for aught but speculative purposes.

'Remarkable!' Lloyd slapped me on the shoulder. 'I should say so. Why, old chap, to coat myself with such a paint would be to put the world at my feet. The secrets of kings and courts would be mine, the machinations of diplomats and politicians, the play of stock-gamblers, the plans of trusts and corporations. I could keep my hand on the inner pulse of things and become the greatest power in the world. And I——' He broke off shortly, then added, 'Well, I have begun my experiments, and I don't mind telling you that I'm right in line for it.'

A laugh from the doorway startled us. Paul Tichlorne was standing there, a smile of mockery on his lips.

'You forget, my dear Lloyd,' he said.

'Forget what?'

'You forget,' Paul went on – 'ah, you forget the shadow.'

I saw Lloyd's face drop, but he answered sneeringly, 'I can carry a sunshade, you know.' Then he turned suddenly and fiercely upon him. 'Look here, Paul, you'll keep out of this if you know what's good for you.'

A rupture seemed imminent, but Paul laughed good-naturedly. 'I wouldn't lay fingers on your dirty pigments. Succeed beyond your most sanguine expectations, yet you will always fetch up against the shadow. You can't get away from it. Now I shall go on the very opposite tack. In the very nature of my proposition the shadow will be eliminated——'

'Transparency!' ejaculated Lloyd, instantly. 'But it can't be achieved.'

'Oh no; of course not.' And Paul shrugged his shoulders and strolled off down the brier-rose path.

This was the beginning of it. Both men attacked the problem with all the tremendous energy for which they were noted, and with a rancour and bitterness that made me tremble for the success of either. Each trusted me to the utmost, and in the long weeks of experimentation that followed I was made a party to both sides, listening to their theorizings and witnessing their demonstrations. Never, by word or sign, did I convey to either the slightest hint of the other's progress, and they respected me for the seal I put upon my lips.

Lloyd Inwood, after prolonged and unintermittent application, when the tension upon his mind and body became too great to bear, had a strange way of obtaining relief. He attended prize-fights. It was at one of these brutal exhibitions, whither he had dragged me in order to tell his latest results, that his theory received striking confirmation.

'Do you see that red-whiskered man?' he asked, pointing across the ring to the fifth tier of seats on the opposite side. 'And do you see the next man to him, the one in the white hat? Well, there is quite a gap between them, is there not?'

'Certainly,' I answered. 'They are a seat apart. The gap is the unoccupied seat.'

He leaned over to me and spoke seriously. 'Between the red-whiskered man and the white-hatted man sits Ben Wasson. You have heard me speak of him. He is the cleverest pugilist of his weight in the country. He is also a Caribbean negro, full-blooded, and the blackest in the United States. He has on a black overcoat buttoned up. I saw him when he came in and took that seat. As soon as he sat down he disappeared. Watch closely; he may smile.'

I was for crossing over to verify Lloyd's statement, but he restrained me. 'Wait,' he said.

I waited and watched, till the red-whiskered man turned his head as though addressing the unoccupied seat; and then, in that empty space, I saw the rolling whites of a pair of eyes and the white double-crescent of two rows of teeth, and for the instant I could make out a negro's face. But with the passing of the smile his visibility passed, and the chair seemed vacant as before.

'Were he perfectly black, you could sit alongside him and not see him,' Lloyd said; and I confess the illustration was apt enough to make me wellnigh convinced.

I visited Lloyd's laboratory a number of times after that, and found him always deep in his search after the absolute black. His experiments covered all sorts of pigments, such as lamp-blacks, tars, carbonized vegetable matters, soots of oils and fats, and the various carbonized animal substances.

'White light is composed of the seven primary colours,' he argued to me. 'But it is itself, of itself, invisible. Only by being reflected from objects do it and the objects become visible. But only that portion of it that is reflected becomes visible. For instance, here is a blue tobacco-box. The white light strikes against it, and, with one exception, all its component colours – violet, indigo, green, yellow, orange, and red – are absorbed. The one exception is *blue*. It is not absorbed, but reflected. Wherefore the tobacco-box gives us a sensation of blueness. We do not see the other colours because they are absorbed. We see only the blue. For the same reason grass is *green*. The green waves of white light are thrown upon our eyes.

'When we paint our houses, we do not apply colour to them,' he said at another time. 'What we do is to apply certain substances that have the property of absorbing from white light all the colours except those that we would have our house appear. When a substance reflects all the colours to the eye, it seems to us white. When it absorbs all the colours, it is black. But, as I said before, we have as yet no perfect black. All the colours are not absorbed. The perfect black, guarding against high lights, will be utterly and absolutely invisible. Look at that, for example.'

He pointed to the palette lying on his work-table. Different shades of black-pigments were brushed on it. One, in particular, I could hardly see. It gave my eyes a blurring sensation, and I rubbed them and looked again.

'That,' he said impressively, 'is the blackest black you or any mortal man ever looked upon. But just you wait, and I'll have a black so black that no mortal man will be able to look upon it – *and see it!*'

On the other hand, I used to find Paul Tichlorne plunged as deeply into the study of light polarization, diffraction, and interference, single and double refraction, and all manner of strange organic compounds.

'Transparency: a state or quality of body which permits all rays of light to pass through,' he defined for me. 'That is what I am seeking. Lloyd blunders up against the shadow with his perfect opaqueness. But I escape it. A transparent body casts no shadow; neither does it reflect light-waves – that is, the perfectly transparent does not. So, avoiding high lights, not only will such a body cast no shadow, but, since it reflects light, it will also be invisible.'

We were standing by the window at another time. Paul was engaged in polishing a number of lenses, which were ranged along the sill. Suddenly, after a pause in the conversation, he said, 'Oh! I've dropped a lens. Stick your head out, old man, and see where it went to.'

Out I started to thrust my head, but a sharp blow on the forehead caused me to recoil. I rubbed my bruised brow and gazed with reproachful inquiry at Paul, who was laughing in gleeful, boyish fashion.

'Well?' he said.

'Well?' I echoed.

'Why don't you investigate?' he demanded. And investigate I did. Before thrusting out my head, my senses, automatically active, had told me there was nothing there, that nothing intervened between me and out-of-doors, that the aperture of the window opening was utterly empty. I stretched forth my hand and felt a hard object, smooth and cool and flat, which my touch, out of its experience, told me to be glass. I looked again, but could see positively nothing.

'White quartzose sand,' Paul rattled off, 'sodic carbonate, slaked lime, cullet, manganese peroxide – there you have it, the finest French plate glass, made by the great St Gobain Company, who made the finest plate glass in the world, and this is the finest piece they ever made. It cost a king's ransom. But look at it! You can't see it. You don't know it's there till you run your head against it.

'Eh, old boy! That's merely an object-lesson – certain elements, in themselves opaque, yet so compounded as to give a resultant body which is transparent. But that is a matter of inorganic chemistry, you say. Very true. But I dare to assert, standing here on my two feet, that in the organic I can duplicate whatever occurs in the inorganic.

'Here!' He held a test-tube between me and the light, and I noted the cloudy or muddy liquid it contained. He emptied the contents of another test-tube into it, and almost instantly it became clear and sparkling.

'Or here!' With quick, nervous movements among his array of test-tubes, he turned a white solution to a wine colour, and a light yellow solution to a dark brown. He dropped a piece of litmus paper into an acid, when it changed instantly to red, and on floating it in an alkali it turned as quickly to blue.

'The litmus paper is still the litmus paper,' he enunciated in the formal manner of the lecturer. 'I have not changed it into something else. Then what did I do? I merely changed the arrangement of its molecules. Where, at first, it absorbed all colours from the light but red, its molecular structure was so changed that it absorbed red and all colours except blue. And so it goes, *ad infinitum*. Now, what I purpose to do is this.' He paused for a space. 'I purpose to seek – ay, and to find – the proper reagents, which, acting upon the living organism, will bring about molecular changes analogous to those you have just witnessed. But these reagents, which I shall find, and for that matter, upon which I already have my hands, will not turn the living body to blue or red or black, but they will turn it to transparency. All light will pass through it. It will be invisible. It will cast no shadow.'

A few weeks later I went hunting with Paul. He had been promising me for some time that I should have the pleasure of shooting over a wonderful dog – the most wonderful dog, in fact, that ever man shot over, so he averred, and continued to aver till my curiosity was aroused. But on the morning in question I was disappointed, for there was no dog in evidence.

'Don't see him about,' Paul remarked unconcernedly, and we set off across the fields.

I could not imagine, at the time, what was ailing me, but I had a feeling of some impending and deadly illness. My nerves were all awry, and, from the astounding tricks they played me, my senses seemed to have run riot. Strange sounds disturbed me. At times I heard the swish-swish of grass being shoved aside, and once the patter of feet across a patch of stony ground.

'Did you hear anything, Paul?' I asked once.

But he shook his head, and thrust his feet steadily forward.

While climbing a fence, I heard the low, eager whine of a dog, apparently from within a couple of feet of me; but on looking about me I saw nothing.

I dropped to the ground, limp and trembling.

'Paul,' I said, 'we had better return to the house. I am afraid I am going to be sick.'

'Nonsense, old man,' he answered. 'The sunshine has gone to your head like wine. You'll be all right. It's famous weather.'

But, passing along a narrow path through a clump of cottonwoods, some object brushed against my legs and I stumbled and nearly fell. I looked with sudden anxiety at Paul.

'What's the matter?' he asked. 'Tripping over your own feet?'

I kept my tongue between my teeth and plodded on, though sore perplexed and thoroughly satisfied that some acute and mysterious malady had attacked my nerves. So far my eyes had escaped; but, when we got to the open fields again, even my vision went back on me. Strange flashes of vari-coloured, rainbow light began to appear and disappear on the path before me. Still, I managed to keep myself in hand, till the vari-coloured lights persisted for a space of fully twenty seconds, dancing and flashing in continuous play. Then I sat down, weak and shaky.

'It's all up with me,' I gasped, covering my eyes with my hands. 'It has attacked my eyes. Paul, take me home.'

But Paul laughed long and loud. 'What did I tell you? – the most wonderful dog, eh? Well, what do you think?'

He turned partly from me and began to whistle. I heard the patter of feet, the panting of a heated animal, and the unmistakable yelp of a dog. Then Paul stooped down and apparently fondled the empty air.

'Here! Give me your fist.'

And he rubbed my hand over the cold nose and jowls of a dog. A dog it certainly was, with the shape and the smooth, short coat of a pointer.

Suffice to say, I speedily recovered my spirits and control. Paul put a collar about the animal's neck and tied his handkerchief to its tail. And then was vouchsafed us the remarkable sight of an empty collar and a waving handkerchief cavorting over the fields. It was something to see that collar and handkerchief pin a bevy of quail in a clump of locusts and remain rigid and immovable till we had flushed the birds.

Now and again the dog emitted the vari-coloured light-flashes I have mentioned. The one thing, Paul explained, which he had not anticipated and which he doubted could be overcome.

'They're a large family,' he said, 'these sun dogs, wind dogs, rainbows, halos, and parhelia. They are produced by refraction of light from mineral and ice crystals, from mist, rain, spray, and no end of things; and I am afraid they are the penalty I must pay for transparency. I escaped Lloyd's shadow only to fetch up against the rainbow flash.'

A couple of days later, before the entrance to Paul's laboratory, I encountered a terrible stench. So overpowering was it that it was easy to discover the source – a mass of putrescent matter on the doorstep which in general outlines resembled a dog.

Paul was startled when he investigated my find. It was his invisible dog, or rather, what had been his invisible dog, for it was now plainly visible. It had been playing about but a few minutes before in all health and strength. Closer examination revealed that the skull had been crushed by some heavy blow. While it was strange that the animal should have been killed, the inexplicable thing was that it should so quickly decay.

'The reagents I injected into its system were harmless,' Paul explained. 'Yet they were powerful, and it appears that when death comes they force practically instantaneous disintegration. Remarkable! Most remarkable! Well, the only thing is not to die. They do not harm so long as one lives. But I do wonder who smashed in that dog's head.'

Light, however, was thrown upon this when a frightened housemaid brought the news that Gaffer Bedshaw had that very morning, not more than an hour back, gone violently insane, and was strapped down at home, in the huntsman's lodge, where he raved of a battle with a ferocious and gigantic beast that he had encountered in the Tichlorne pasture. He claimed that the thing, whatever it was, was invisible, that with his own eyes he had seen that it was invisible; wherefore his tearful wife and daughters shook their heads, and wherefore he but waxed the more violent, and the gardener and the coachman tightened the straps by another hole.

Nor, while Paul Tichlorne was thus successfully mastering the problem of invisibility, was Lloyd Inwood a whit behind. I went over in answer to a message of his to come and see how he was getting on. Now his laboratory occupied an isolated situation in the midst of his vast grounds. It was built in a pleasant little glade, surrounded on all sides by a dense forest growth, and was to be gained by way of a winding and erratic path. But I had travelled that path so often as to know every foot of it, and conceive my surprise when I came upon the glade and found no laboratory. The quaint shed structure with its red sandstone chimney was not. Nor did it look as if it ever had been. There were no signs of ruin, no debris, nothing.

I started to walk across what had once been its site. 'This,' I said to myself, 'should be where the step went up to the door.' Barely were the words out of my mouth when I stubbed my toe on some obstacle, pitched forward, and butted my head into something that *felt* very much like a door. I reached out my hand. It *was* a door. I found the knob and turned it. And at once, as the door swung inward on its hinges, the whole interior of the laboratory impinged itself upon my vision. Greeting Lloyd, I closed the door and backed up the path a few paces. I could see nothing of the building. Returning and opening the door, at once all the furniture and every detail of the interior were visible. It was indeed startling, the sudden transition from void to light and form and colour.

'What do you think of it, eh?' Lloyd asked, wringing my hand. 'I slapped a couple of coats of absolute black on the outside yesterday afternoon to see how it worked. How's your head? You bumped it pretty solidly, I imagine.'

'Never mind that,' he interrupted my congratulations. 'I've something better for you to do.'

While he talked he began to strip, and when he stood naked before me he thrust a pot and brush into my hand and said, 'Here, give me a coat of this.'

It was an oily, shellac-like stuff, which spread quickly and easily over the skin and dried immediately.

'Merely preliminary and precautionary,' he explained when I had finished; 'but now for the real stuff.'

I picked up another pot he indicated, and glanced inside, but could see nothing.

'It's empty,' I said.

'Stick your finger in it.'

I obeyed, and was aware of a sensation of cool moistness. On withdrawing my hand I glanced at the forefinger, the one I had immersed, but it had disappeared. I moved it, and knew from the alternate tension and relaxation of the muscles that I moved it, but it defied my sense of sight. To all appearances I had been shorn of a finger; nor could I get any visual impression of it till I extended it under the skylight and saw its shadow plainly blotted on the floor.

Lloyd chuckled. 'Now spread it on, and keep your eyes open.'

I dipped the brush into the seemingly empty pot, and gave him a long stroke across his chest. With the passage of the brush the living flesh disappeared from beneath. I covered his right leg, and he was a one-legged man defying all laws of gravitation. And so, stroke by stroke, member by member, I painted Lloyd Inwood into nothingness. It was a creepy experience, and I was glad when naught remained in sight but his burning black eyes, poised apparently unsupported in mid-air.

'I have a refined and harmless solution for them,' he said. 'A fine spray with an air-brush, and presto! I am not.'

This deftly accomplished, he said, 'Now I shall move about and do you tell me what sensations you experience.'

'In the first place I cannot see you,' I said, and I could hear his gleeful laugh from the midst of the emptiness. 'Of course,' I continued, 'you cannot escape your shadow, but that was to be expected. When you pass between my eyes and an object, the object disappears, but so unusual and incomprehensible is its disappearance that it seems to me as though my eyes had blurred. When you move rapidly, I experience a bewildering succession of blurs. The blurring sensation makes my eyes ache and my brain tired.'

'Have you any other warnings of my presence?' he asked.

'No, and yes,' I answered. 'When you are near me I have feelings similar to those produced by dank warehouses, gloomy crypts, and deep mines. And as sailors feel the loom of the land on dark nights, so I think I feel the loom of your body. But it is all very vague and intangible.'

Long we talked that last morning in his laboratory; and when I turned to go, he put his unseen hand in mine with nervous grip, and said, 'Now I shall conquer the world!' And I could not dare to tell him of Paul Tichlorne's equal success.

At home I found a note from Paul, asking me to come up immediately, and it was high noon when I came spinning up the driveway on my wheel. Paul called me from the tennis court, and I dismounted and went over. But the court was empty. I stood there, gaping open-mouthed, a tennis ball struck me on the arm, and as I turned about, another whizzed past my ear. For aught I could see of my assailant, they came whirling at me from out of space, and right well was I peppered with them. But when the balls already flung at me began to come back for a second whack, I realized the situation. Seizing a racquet and keeping my eyes open, I quickly saw a rainbow flash appearing and disappearing and darting over the ground. I took out after it, and when I laid the racquet upon it for half-a-dozen stout blows, Paul's voice rang out:

'Enough! Enough! Oh! Ouch! Stop! You're landing on my naked skin, you know! Ow! Ow-w-w! I'll be good! I'll be good! I only wanted you to see my metamorphosis,' he said ruefully, and I imagined he was rubbing his hurts.

A few minutes later we were playing tennis – a handicap on my part, for I could have no knowledge of his position save when all the angles between himself, the sun, and me, were in proper conjunction. Then he flashed, and only then. But the flashes were more brilliant than the rainbow – purest blue, most delicate violet, brightest yellow, and all the intermediary shades, with the scintillant brilliancy of the diamond, dazzling, blinding iridescent.

But in the midst of our play I felt a sudden cold chill, reminding me of deep mines and gloomy crypts, such a chill as I had experienced that very morning. The next moment, close to the net, I saw a ball rebound in mid-air and empty space, and at the same instant, a score of feet away, Paul Tichlorne emitted a rainbow flash. It could not be he from whom the ball had rebounded, and with sickening dread I realized that Lloyd Inwood had come upon the scene. To make sure, I looked for his shadow, and there it was, a shapeless blotch and girth of his body (the sun was overhead), moving along the ground. I remembered his threat, and felt sure that all the long years of rivalry were about to culminate in uncanny battle.

I cried a warning to Paul, and heard a snarl as of a wild beast, and an answering snarl. I saw the dark blotch move swiftly across the court, and a brilliant burst of vari-coloured light moving with equal swiftness to meet it; and then shadow and flash came together and there was the sound of unseen blows. The net went down before my frightened eyes. I sprang towards the fighters, crying:

'For God's sake!'

But their locked bodies smote against my knees, and I was overthrown.

'You keep out of this, old man!' I heard the voice of Lloyd Inwood from out of the emptiness. And then Paul's voice crying, 'Yes, we've had enough of peacemaking!'

From the sound of their voices I knew they had separated. I could not locate Paul, and so approached the shadow that represented Lloyd. But from the other side came a stunning blow on the point of my jaw, and I heard Paul scream angrily, 'Now will you keep away?'

Then they came together again, the impact of their blows, their groans and gasps, and the swift flashings and shadow-movings telling plainly of the deadliness of the struggle.

I shouted for help, and Gaffer Bedshaw came running into the court. I could see, as he approached, that he was looking at me strangely, but he collided with the combatants and was hurled headlong to the ground. With despairing shriek and a cry of 'O Lord, I've got 'em!' he sprang to his feet and tore out of the court.

I could do nothing, so I sat up, fascinated and powerless, and watched the struggle. The noonday sun beat down with dazzling brightness on the naked tennis court. And it *was* naked. All I could see was the invisible feet, the earth tearing up from beneath the straining foot-grips, and the wire screen bulge once or twice as their bodies hurled against it. That was all, and after a time even that ceased. There were no more flashes, and the shadow had become long and stationary; and I remembered their set boyish faces when they clung to the roots in the deep coolness of the pool.

They found me an hour afterwards. Some inkling of what had happened got to the servants and they quitted the Tichlorne service in a body. Gaffer Bedshaw never recovered from the second shock he received, and is confined in a madhouse, hopelessly incurable. The secrets of their marvellous discoveries died with Paul and Lloyd, both laboratories being destroyed by grief-stricken relatives. As for myself, I no longer care for chemical research, and science is a tabooed topic in my household. I have returned to my roses. Nature's colours are good enough for me.

THE UNPARALLELED INVASION

It was in the year 1976 that the trouble between the world and China reached its culmination. It was because of this that the celebration of the Second Centennial of American Liberty was deferred. Many other plans of the nations of the earth were twisted and tangled and postponed for the same reason. The world awoke rather abruptly to its danger; but for over seventy years, unperceived, affairs had been shaping towards this very end.

The year 1904 logically marks the beginning of the development that, seventy years later, was to bring consternation to the whole world. The Japanese-Russian War took place in 1904, and the historians of the time gravely noted it down that that event marked the entrance of Japan into the comity of nations. What it really did mark was the awakening of China. This awakening, long expected, had finally been given up. The Western nations had tried to arouse China, and they had failed. Out of their native optimism and race-egoism they had therefore concluded that the task was impossible, that China would never awaken.

What they had failed to take into account was this: *that between them and China was no common psychological speech*. Their thought-processes were radically dissimilar. There was no intimate vocabulary. The Western mind penetrated the Chinese mind but a short distance when it found itself in a fathomless maze. The Chinese mind penetrated the Western mind an equally short distance when it fetched up against a blank, incomprehensible wall. It was all a matter of language. There was no way to communicate Western ideas to the Chinese mind. China remained asleep. The material achievement and progress of the West was a closed book to her; nor could the West open the book. Back and deep down on the tie-ribs of consciousness, in the mind, say, of the English-speaking race, was a capacity to thrill to short, Saxon words; back and deep down on the tie-ribs of consciousness of the Chinese mind was a capacity to thrill to its own hieroglyphics; but the Chinese mind could not thrill to short, Saxon words; nor could the English-speaking mind thrill to hieroglyphics. The fabrics of their minds were woven from totally different stuffs. They were mental aliens. And so it was that Western material achievement and progress made no dent on the rounded sleep of China.

Came Japan and her victory over Russia in 1904. Now the Japanese race was the freak and paradox among Eastern peoples. In some strange way Japan was receptive to all the West had to offer. Japan swiftly assimilated the Western ideas, and digested them, and so capably applied them that she suddenly burst forth, full-panoplied, a world-power. There is no explaining this peculiar openness of Japan to the alien culture of the West. As well might be explained any biological sport in the animal kingdom.

Having decisively thrashed the great Russian Empire, Japan promptly set about dreaming a colossal dream of empire for herself. Korea she had made into a granary and a colony; treaty privileges and vulpine diplomacy gave her the monopoly of Manchuria. But Japan was not satisfied. She turned her eyes upon China. There lay a vast territory, and in that territory were the hugest deposits in the world of iron and coal – the backbone of industrial civilization. Given natural resources, the other great factor in industry is labour. In that territory was a population of 400,000,000 souls – one quarter of the then total population of the earth. Furthermore, the Chinese were excellent workers, while their fatalistic philosophy (or religion) and their stolid nervous organization constituted them splendid soldiers – if they were properly managed. Needless to say, Japan was prepared to furnish that management.

But best of all, from the standpoint of Japan, the Chinese was a kindred race. The baffling enigma of the Chinese character to the West was no baffling enigma to the Japanese. The Japanese understood as we could never school ourselves or hope to understand. Their mental processes were the same. The Japanese thought with the same thought symbols as the Chinese, and they thought in the same peculiar grooves. Into the Chinese mind the Japanese went on where we were balked by the obstacle of incomprehension. They took the turning which we could not perceive, twisted around the obstacle, and were out of sight in the ramifications of the Chinese mind where we could not follow. They were brothers. Long ago one had borrowed the other's written language, and, untold generations before that, they had diverged from the common Mongol stock. There had been changes, differentiations brought about by diverse conditions and infusions of other blood; but down at the bottom of their beings, twisted into the fibres of them, was a heritage in common, a sameness in kind that time had not obliterated.

And so Japan took upon herself the management of China. In the years immediately following the war with Russia, her agents swarmed over the Chinese Empire. A thousand miles beyond the last mission station toiled her engineers and spies, clad as coolies, under the guise of itinerant merchants or proselytizing Buddhist priests, noting down the horse-power of every waterfall, the likely sites for factories, the heights of mountains and passes, the strategic advantages and weaknesses, the wealth of the farming valleys, the number of bullocks in a district or the number of labourers that could be collected by forced levies. Never was there such a census, and it could have been taken by no other people than the dogged, patient, patriotic Japanese.

But in a short time secrecy was thrown to the winds. Japan's officers reorganized the Chinese army; her drill sergeants made the medieval warriors over into twentieth-century soldiers, accustomed to all the modern machinery of war and with a higher average of marksmanship than the soldiers of any Western nation. The engineers of Japan deepened and widened the intricate system of canals, built factories and foundries, netted the empire with telegraphs and telephones, and inaugurated the era of railroad-building. It was these same protagonists of machine-civilization that discovered the great oil deposits of Chunsan, the iron mountains of Whang-Sing, the copper ranges of Chinchi, and they sank the gas wells of Wow-Wee, that most marvellous reservoir of natural gas in all the world.

In China's councils of empire were the Japanese emissaries. In the ears of the statesmen whispered the Japanese statesmen. The political reconstruction of the Empire was due to them. They evicted the scholar class, which was violently reactionary, and put into office progressive officials. And in every town and city of the Empire newspapers were started. Of course, Japanese editors ran the policy of these papers, which policy they got direct from Tokio. It was these papers that educated and made progressive the great mass of the population.

China was at last awake. Where the West had failed, Japan succeeded. She had transmuted Western culture and achievement into terms that were intelligible to the Chinese understanding. Japan herself, when she so suddenly awakened, had astounded the world. But at the time she was only forty millions strong. China's awakening, with her four hundred millions and the scientific advance of the world, was frightfully astounding. She was the colossus of the nations, and swiftly her voice was heard in no uncertain tones in the affairs and councils of the nations. Japan egged her on, and the proud Western peoples listened with respectful ears.

China's swift and remarkable rise was due, perhaps more than to anything else, to the superlative quality of her labour. The Chinese was the perfect type of industry. He had always been that. For sheer ability to work no worker in the world could compare with him. Work was the breath of his nostrils. It was to him what wandering and fighting in far lands and spiritual adventure had been to other peoples. Liberty, to him, epitomized itself in access to the means of toil. To till the soil and labour interminably was all he asked of life and the powers that be. And the awakening of China had given its vast population not merely free and unlimited access to the means of toil, but access to the highest and most scientific machine-means of toil.

China rejuvenescent! It was but a step to China rampant. She discovered a new pride in herself and a will of her own. She began to chafe under the guidance of Japan, but she did not chafe long. On Japan's advice, in the beginning, she had expelled from the Empire all Western missionaries, engineers, drill sergeants, merchants, and teachers. She now began to expel the similar representatives of Japan. The latter's advisory statesmen were showered with honours and decorations, and sent home. The West had awakened Japan, and, as Japan had then requited the West, Japan was now requited by China. Japan was thanked for her kindly aid and flung out bag and baggage by her gigantic protégé. The Western nations chuckled. Japan's rainbow dream had gone glimmering. She grew angry. China laughed at her. The blood and the swords of the Samurai would out, and Japan rashly went to war. This occurred in 1922, and in seven bloody months Manchuria, Korea, and Formosa were taken away from her and she was hurled back, bankrupt, to stifle in her tiny, crowded islands. Exit Japan from the world drama. Thereafter she devoted herself to art, and her task became to please the world greatly with her creations of wonder and beauty.

Contrary to expectation, China did not prove warlike. She had no Napoleonic dream, and was content to devote herself to the arts of peace. After a time of disquiet, the idea was accepted that China was to be feared, not in war, but in commerce. It will be seen that the real danger was not apprehended. China went on consummating her machine-civilization. Instead of a large standing army, she developed an immensely larger and splendidly efficient militia. Her navy was so small that it was the laughing-stock of the world; nor did she attempt to strengthen her navy. The treaty ports of the world were never entered by her visiting battleships.

The real danger lay in the fecundity of her loins, and it was in 1970 that the first cry of alarm was raised. For some time all territories adjacent to China had been grumbling at Chinese immigration; but now it suddenly came home to the world that China's population was 500,000,000. She had increased by a hundred millions since her awakening. Burchaldter called attention to the fact that there were more Chinese in existence than white-skinned people. He performed a simple sum in arithmetic. He added together the populations of the United States, Canada, New Zealand, Australia, South Africa, England, France, Germany, Italy, Austria, European Russia, and all Scandinavia. The result was 495,000,000. And the population of China overtopped this tremendous total by 5,000,000. Burchaldter's figures went round the world, and the world shivered.

For many centuries China's population had been constant. Her territory had been saturated with population; that is to say, her territory, with the primitive method of production, had supported the maximum limit of population. But when she awoke and inaugurated the machine-civilization, her productive power had been enormously increased. Thus on the same territory, she was able to support a far larger population. At once the birth rate began to rise and the death rate to fall. Before, when population pressed against the means of subsistence, the excess population had been swept away by famine. But now, thanks to the machine-civilization, China's means of subsistence had been enormously extended, and there were no famines; her population followed on the heels of the increase in the means of subsistence.

During this time of transition and development of power, China had entertained no dreams of conquest. The Chinese was not an imperial race. It was industrious, thrifty, and peace-loving. War was looked upon as an unpleasant but necessary task that at times must be performed. And so, while the Western races had squabbled and fought, and world-adventured against one another, China had calmly gone on working at her machines and growing. Now she was spilling over the boundaries of her Empire — that was all, just spilling over into the adjacent territories with all the certainty and terrifying slow momentum of a glacier.

Following upon the alarm raised by Burchaldter's figures, in 1970, France made a long-threatened stand. French Indo-China had been over-run, filled up, by Chinese immigrants. France called a halt. The Chinese wave flowed on. France assembled a force of a hundred thousand on the boundary between her unfortunate colony and China, and China sent down an army of militia-soldiers a million strong. Behind came the wives and sons and daughters and relatives, with their personal household luggage, in a second army. The French force was brushed aside like a fly. The Chinese militia-soldiers, along with their families, over five millions all told, coolly took possession of French Indo-China and settled down to stay for a few thousand years.

Outraged France was in arms. She hurled fleet after fleet against the coast of China, and nearly bankrupted herself by the effort. China had no navy. She withdrew like a turtle into her shell. For a year the French fleets blockaded the coast and bombarded exposed towns and villages. China did not mind. She did not depend upon the rest of the world for anything. She calmly kept out of range of the French guns and went on working. France wept and wailed, wrung her impotent hands and appealed to the dumbfounded nations. Then she landed a punitive expedition to march to Peking. It was two hundred and fifty thousand strong, and it was the flower of France. It landed without opposition and marched into the interior. And that was the last ever seen of it. The line of communication was snapped on the second day. Not a survivor came back to tell what had happened. It had been swallowed up in China's cavernous maw, that was all.

In the five years that followed, China's expansion, in all land directions, went on apace. Siam was made part of the Empire, and, in spite of all that England could do, Burma and the Malay Peninsula were overrun; while all along the long south boundary of Siberia, Russia was pressed severely by China's advancing hordes. The process was simple. First came the Chinese immigration (or, rather, it was already there, having come there slowly and insidiously during the previous years). Next came the clash of arms and the brushing away of all opposition by a monster army of militia-soldiers, followed by their families and household baggage. And finally came their settling down as colonists in the conquered territory. Never was there so strange and effective a method of world conquest.

Nepal and Bhutan were overrun, and the whole northern boundary of India pressed against by this fearful tide of life. To the west, Bokhara, and, even to the south and west, Afghanistan, were swallowed up. Persia, Turkestan, and all Central Asia felt the pressure of the flood. It was at this time that Burchaldter revised his figures. He had been mistaken. China's population must be seven hundred millions, eight hundred millions, nobody knew how many millions, but at any rate it would soon be a billion. There were two Chinese for every white-skinned human in the world, Burchaldter announced, and the world trembled. China's increase must have begun immediately, in 1904. It was remembered that since that date there had not been a single famine. At 5,000,000 a year increase, her total increase in the intervening seventy years must be 350,000,000. But who was to know? It might be more. Who was to know anything of this strange new menace of the twentieth century – China, old China, rejuvenescent, fruitful, and militant!

The Convention of 1975 was called at Philadelphia. All the Western nations, and some few of the Eastern, were represented. Nothing was accomplished. There was talk of all countries putting bounties on children to increase the birth rate, but it was laughed to scorn by the arithmeticians, who pointed out that China was too far in the lead in that direction. No feasible way of coping with China was suggested. China was appealed to and threatened by the United Powers, and that was all the Convention of Philadelphia came to; and the Convention and the Powers were laughed at by China. Li Tang Fwung, the power behind the Dragon Throne, deigned to reply.

'What does China care for the comity of nations?' said Li Tang Fwung. 'We are the most ancient, honourable, and royal of races. We have our own destiny to accomplish. It is unpleasant that our destiny does not tally with the destiny of the rest of the world, but what would you? You have talked windily about the royal races and the heritage of the earth, and we can only reply that that remains to be seen. You cannot invade us. Never mind about your navies. Don't shout. We know our navy is small. You see, we use it for police purposes. We do not care for the sea. Our strength is in our population, which will soon be a billion. Thanks to you, we are equipped with all modern war-machinery. Send your navies. We will not notice them. Send your punitive expeditions, but first remember France. To land half a million soldiers on our shores would strain the resources of any of you. And our thousand millions would swallow them down in a mouthful. Send a million; send five millions, and we will swallow them down just as readily. Pouf! A mere nothing, a meagre morsel. Destroy, as you have threatened, you United States, the ten million coolies we have forced upon your shores – why, the amount scarcely equals half of our excess birth rate for a year.'

So spoke Li Tang Fwung. The world was nonplussed, helpless, terrified. Truly had he spoken. There was no combating China's amazing birth rate. If her population was a billion, and was increasing twenty millions a year, in twenty-five years it would be a billion and a half – equal to the total population of the world in 1904. And nothing could be done. There was no way to dam up the over-spilling monstrous flood of life. War was futile. China laughed at a blockade of her coasts. She welcomed invasion. In her capacious maw was room for all the hosts of earth that could be hurled at her. And in the meantime her flood of yellow life poured out and on over Asia. China laughed and read in their magazines the learned lucubrations of the distracted Western scholars.

But there was one scholar China failed to reckon on – Jacobus Laningdale. Not that he was a scholar, except in the widest sense. Primarily, Jacobus Laningdale was a scientist, and, up to that time, a very obscure scientist, a professor employed in the laboratories of the Health Office of New York City. Jacobus Laningdale's head was very like any other head, but in that head was evolved an idea. Also, in that head was the wisdom to keep that idea secret. He did not write an article for the magazines. Instead, he asked for a vacation. On September 19, 1975, he arrived in Washington. It was evening, but he proceeded straight to the White House, for he had already arranged an audience with the President. He was closeted with President Moyer for three hours. What passed between them was not learned by the rest of the world until long after; in fact, at that time the world was not interested in Jacobus Laningdale. Next day the President called in his Cabinet. Jacobus Laningdale was present. The proceedings were kept secret. But that very afternoon Rufus Cowdery, Secretary of State, left Washington, and early the following morning sailed for England. The secret that he carried began to spread, but it spread only among the heads of Governments.

Possibly half-a-dozen men in a nation were entrusted with the idea that had formed in Jacobus Laningdale's head. Following the spread of the secret, sprang up great activity in all the dockyards, arsenals, and navy-yards. The people of France and Austria became suspicious, but so sincere were their Governments' calls for confidence that they acquiesced in the unknown project that was afoot.

This was the time of the Great Truce. All countries pledged themselves solemnly not to go to war with any other country. The first definite action was the gradual mobilization of the armies of Russia, Germany, Austria, Italy, Greece, and Turkey. Then began the eastward movement. All railroads into Asia were glutted with troop trains. China was the objective, that was all that was known. A little later began the great sea movement. Expeditions of warships were launched from all countries. Fleet followed fleet, and all proceeded to the coast of China. The nations cleaned out their navy-yards. They sent their revenue cutters and dispatch boats and lighthouse tenders, and they sent their last antiquated cruisers and battleships. Not content with this, they impressed the merchant marine. The statistics show that 58,640 merchant steamers, equipped with searchlights and rapid-fire guns, were dispatched by the various nations to China.

And China smiled and waited. On her land side, along her boundaries, were millions of the warriors of Europe. She mobilized five times as many millions of her militia and awaited the invasion. On her sea coasts she did the same. But China was puzzled. After all this enormous preparation, there was no invasion. She could not understand. Along the great Siberian frontier all was quiet. Along her coasts the towns and villages were not even shelled. Never, in the history of the world, had there been so mighty a gathering of war fleets. The fleets of all the world were there, and day and night millions of tons of battleships ploughed the brine of her coasts, and nothing happened. Nothing was attempted. Did they think to make her emerge from her shell? China smiled. Did they think to tire her out, or starve her out? China smiled again.

But on May 1, 1976, had the reader been in the imperial city of Peking, with its then population of eleven millions, he would have witnessed a curious sight. He would have seen the streets filled with the chattering yellow populace, every queued head tilted back, every slant eye turned skyward. And high up in the blue he would have beheld a tiny dot of black, which, because of its orderly evolutions, he would have identified as an airship. From this airship, as it curved its flight back and forth over the city, fell missiles — strange, harmless missiles, tubes of fragile glass that shattered into tiny thousands of fragments on the streets and house-tops. But there was nothing deadly about these tubes of glass. Nothing happened. There were no explosions. It is true, three Chinese were killed by the tubes dropping on their heads from so enormous a height; but what were three Chinese against an excess birth rate of twenty millions? One tube struck perpendicularly in a fish-pond in a garden and was not broken. It was dragged ashore by the master of the house. He did not dare to open it, but, accompanied by his friends, and surrounded by an ever-increasing crowd, he carried the mysterious tube to the magistrate of the district. The latter was a brave man. With all eyes upon him, he shattered the tube with a blow from his brass-bowled pipe. Nothing happened. Of those who were very near, one or two thought they saw some mosquitoes fly out. That was all. The crowd set up a great laugh and dispersed.

As Peking was bombarded by glass tubes, so was all China. The tiny airships, dispatched from the warships, contained but two men each, and over all cities, towns, and villages they wheeled and curved, one man directing the ship, the other man throwing over the glass tubes.

Had the reader again been in Peking, six weeks later, he would have looked in vain for the eleven million inhabitants. Some few of them he would have found, a few hundred thousand, perhaps, their carcases festering in the houses and in the deserted streets, and piled high on the abandoned death-wagons. But for the rest he would have had to seek along the highways and byways of the Empire. And not all would he have found fleeing from plague-stricken Peking, for behind them, by hundreds of thousands of unburied corpses by the wayside, he could have marked their flight. And as it was with Peking, so it was with all the cities, towns, and villages of the Empire. The plague smote them all. Nor was it one plague, nor two plagues; it was a score of plagues. Every virulent form of infectious death stalked through the land. Too late the Chinese government apprehended the meaning of the colossal preparations, the marshalling of the world-hosts, the flights of the tiny airships, and the rain of the tubes of glass. The proclamations of the government were vain. They could not stop the eleven million plague-stricken wretches, fleeing from the one city of Peking to spread disease through all the land. The physicians and health officers died at their posts; and death, the all-conqueror, rode over the decrees of the Emperor and Li Tang Fwung. It rode over them as well, for Li Tang Fwung died in the second week, and the Emperor, hidden away in the Summer Palace, died in the fourth week.

Had there been one plague, China might have coped with it. But from a score of plagues no creature was immune. The man who escaped smallpox went down before scarlet fever. The man who was immune to yellow fever was carried away by cholera; and if he were immune to that, too, the Black Death, which was the bubonic plague, swept him away. For it was these bacteria, and germs, and microbes, and bacilli, cultured in the laboratories of the West, that had come down upon China in the rain of glass.

All organization vanished. The government crumbled away. Decrees and proclamations were useless when the men who made them and signed them one moment were dead the next. Nor could the maddened millions, spurred on to flight by death, pause to heed anything. They fled from the cities to infect the country, and wherever they fled they carried the plagues with them. The hot summer was on — Jacobus Laningdale had selected the time shrewdly — and the plague festered everywhere. Much is conjectured of what occurred, and much has been learned from the stories of the few survivors. The wretched creatures stormed across the Empire in many-millioned flight. The vast armies China had collected on her frontiers melted away. The farms were ravaged for food, and no more crops were planted, while the crops already in were left unattended and never came to harvest. The most remarkable thing, perhaps, was the flights. Many millions engaged in them, charging to the bounds of the Empire to be met and turned back by the gigantic armies of the West. The slaughter of the mad hosts on the boundaries was stupendous. Time and again the guarding line was drawn back twenty or thirty miles to escape the contagion of the multitudinous dead.

Once the plague broke through and seized upon the German and Austrian soldiers who were guarding the borders of Turkestan. Preparations had been made for such a happening, and though sixty thousand soldiers of Europe were carried off, the international corps of physicians isolated the contagion and dammed it back. It was during this struggle that it was suggested that a new plague-germ had originated, that in some way or other a sort of hybridization between plague-germs had taken place, producing a new and frightfully virulent germ. First suspected by Vomberg, who became infected with it and died, it was later isolated and studied by Stevens, Hazenfelt, Norman, and Landers.

Such was the unparalleled invasion of China. For that billion of people there was no hope. Pent in their vast and festering charnel-house, all organization and cohesion lost, they could do naught but die. They could not escape. As they were flung back from their land frontiers, so were they flung back from the sea. Seventy-five thousand vessels patrolled the coasts. By day their smoking funnels dimmed the sea-rim, and by night their flashing searchlights ploughed the dark and harrowed it for the tiniest escaping junk. The attempts of the immense fleets of junks were pitiful. Not one ever got by the guarding sea-hounds. Modern war-machinery held back the disorganized mass of China, while the plagues did the work.

But old War was made a thing of laughter. Naught remained to him but patrol duty. China had laughed at war, and war she was getting, but it was ultra-modern war, twentieth century war, the war of the scientist and the laboratory, the war of Jacobus Laningdale. Hundred-ton guns were toys compared with the micro-organic projectiles hurled from the laboratories, the messengers of death, the destroying angels that stalked through the empire of a billion souls.

During all the summer and fall of 1976 China was an inferno. There was no eluding the microscopic projectiles that sought out the remotest hiding-places. The hundreds of millions of dead remained unburied and the germs multiplied themselves, and, towards the last, millions died daily of starvation. Besides, starvation weakened the victims and destroyed their natural defences against the plagues. Cannibalism, murder, and madness reigned. And so perished China.

Not until the following February, in the coldest weather, were the first expeditions made. These expeditions were small, composed of scientists and bodies of troops; but they entered China from every side. In spite of the most elaborate precautions against infection, numbers of soldiers and a few of the physicians were stricken. But the exploration went bravely on. They found China devastated, a howling wilderness through which wandered bands of wild dogs and desperate bandits who had survived. All survivors were put to death wherever found. And then began the great task, the sanitation of China. Five years and hundreds of millions of treasure were consumed, and then the world moved in – not in zones, as was the idea of Baron Albrecht, but heterogeneously, according to the democratic American programme. It was a vast and happy intermingling of nationalities that settled down in China in 1982 and the years that followed – a tremendous and successful experiment in cross-fertilization. We know today the splendid mechanical, intellectual, and art output that followed.

It was in 1987, the Great Truce having been dissolved, that the ancient quarrel between France and Germany over Alsace-Lorraine recrudesced. The war-cloud grew dark and threatening in April, and on April 17 the Convention of Copenhagen was called. The representatives of the nations of the world being present, all nations solemnly pledged themselves never to use against one another the laboratory methods of warfare they had employed in the invasion of China.

THE HEATHEN

I met him first in a hurricane; and though we had gone through the hurricane on the same schooner, it was not until the schooner had gone to pieces under us that I first laid eyes on him. Without doubt I had seen him with the rest of the Kanaka crew on board, but I had not consciously been aware of his existence, for the *Petite Jeanne* was rather overcrowded. In addition to her eight or ten Kanaka seamen, her white captain, mate, and supercargo, and her six cabin passengers, she sailed from Rangiroa with something like eighty-five deck passengers – Paumotans and Tahitians, men, women, and children each with a trade box, to say nothing of sleeping mats, blankets, and clothes bundles.

The pearling season in the Paumotas was over, and all hands were returning to Tahiti. The six of us cabin passengers were pearl buyers. Two were Americans, one was Ah Choon (the whitest Chinese I have ever known), one was a German, one was a Polish Jew, and I completed the half dozen.

It had been a prosperous season. Not one of us had cause for complaint, nor one of the eighty-five deck passengers either. All had done well, and all were looking forward to a rest-off and a good time in Papeete.

Of course the *Petite Jeanne* was overloaded. She was only seventy tons, and she had no right to carry a tithe of the mob she had on board. Beneath her hatches she was crammed and jammed with pearl shell and copra. Even the trade room was packed full with shell. It was a miracle that the sailors could work her. There was no moving about the decks. They simply climbed back and forth along the rails.

In the night-time they walked upon the sleepers, who carpeted the deck, I'll swear, two deep. Oh, and there were pigs and chickens on deck, and sacks of yams, while every conceivable place was festooned with strings of drinking coconuts and bunches of bananas. On both sides, between the fore and main shrouds, guys had been stretched, just low enough for the foreboom to swing clear; and from each of these guys at least fifty bunches of bananas were suspended.

It promised to be a messy passage, even if we did make it in the two or three days that would have been required if the south-east trades had been blowing fresh. But they weren't blowing fresh. After the first five

hours the trade died away in a dozen or so gasping fans. The calm
continued all that night and the next day – one of those glaring, glassy
calms, when the very thought of opening one's eyes to look at it is
sufficient to cause a headache.

The second day a man died – an Easter Islander, one of the best divers
that season in the lagoon. Smallpox – that is what it was; though how
smallpox could come on board, when there had been no known cases
ashore when we left Rangiroa, is beyond me. There it was, though –
smallpox, a man dead, and three others down on their backs.

There was nothing to be done. We could not segregate the sick, nor
could we care for them. We were packed like sardines. There was
nothing to do but rot and die – that is, there was nothing to do after the
night that followed the first death. On that night the mate, the
supercargo, the Polish Jew, and four native divers sneaked away in the
large whale-boat. They were never heard of again. In the morning the
captain promptly scuttled the remaining boats, and there we were.

That day there were two deaths; the following day three; then it
jumped to eight. It was curious to see how we took it. The natives, for
instance, fell into a condition of dumb, stolid fear. The captain –
Oudouse, his name was, a Frenchman – became very nervous and
voluble. He actually got the twitches. He was a large, fleshy man,
weighing at least two hundred pounds, and he quickly became a faithful
representation of a quivering jelly mountain of fat.

The German, the two Americans, and myself bought up all the scotch
whisky and proceeded to stay drunk. The theory was beautiful – namely,
if we kept ourselves soaked in alcohol, every smallpox germ that came
into contact with us would immediately be scorched to a cinder. And the
theory worked, though I must confess that neither Captain Oudouse nor
Ah Choon was attacked by the disease either. The Frenchman did not
drink at all, while Ah Choon restricted himself to one drink daily.

It was a pretty time. The sun, going into northern declination, was
straight overhead. There was no wind, except for frequent squalls, which
blew fiercely for from five minutes to half an hour, and wound up by
deluging us with rain. After each squall the awful sun would come out,
drawing clouds of steam from the soaked decks.

The steam was not nice. It was the vapour of death, freighted with
millions and millions of germs. We always took another drink when we
saw it going up from the dead and dying, and usually we took two or
three more drinks, mixing them exceptionally stiff. Also we made it a
rule to take an additional several each time they hove the dead over to
the sharks that swarmed about us.

We had a week of it, and then the whisky gave out. It is just as well, or
I shouldn't be alive now. It took a sober man to pull through what

followed, as you will agree when I mention the little fact that only two men did pull through. The other man was the heathen – at least, that was what I heard Captain Oudouse call him at the moment I first became aware of the heathen's existence. But to come back.

It was at the end of the week, with the whisky gone and the pearl buyers sober, that I happened to glance at the barometer that hung in the cabin companion-way. Its normal register in the Paumotas was 29.90, and it was quite customary to see it vacillate between 29.85 and 30.00, or even 30.05; but to see it as I saw it, down to 29.62, was sufficient to sober the most drunken pearl buyer that ever incinerated smallpox microbes in scotch whisky.

I called Captain Oudouse's attention to it, only to be informed that he had watched it going down for several hours. There was little to do, but that little he did very well, considering the circumstances. He took off the light sails, shortened right down to storm canvas, spread life lines, and waited for the wind. His mistake lay in what he did after the wind came. He hove to on the port tack, which was the right thing to do south of the Equator if – and there was the rub – *if* one were *not* in the direct path of the hurricane.

We were in the direct path. I could see that by the steady increase of the wind and the equally steady fall of the barometer. I wanted him to turn and run with the wind on the port quarters until the barometer ceased falling, and then to heave to. We argued till he was reduced to hysteria, but budge he would not. The worst of it was that I could not get the rest of the pearl buyers to back me up. Who was I, anyway, to know more about the sea and its ways than a properly qualified captain? was what was in their minds, I knew.

Of course the sea rose with the wind frightfully; and I shall never forget the first three seas the *Petite Jeanne* shipped. She had fallen off, as vessels do at times when hove to, and the first sea made a clean breach. The life lines were only for the strong and well, and little good were they even for them when the women and children, the bananas and coconuts, the pigs and trade boxes, the sick and the dying, were swept along in a solid, screeching, groaning mass.

The second sea filled the *Petite Jeanne*'s deck flush with the rails; and as her stern sank down and her bow tossed skyward, all the miserable dunnage of life and luggage poured aft. It was a human torrent. They came head first, feet first, sideways, rolling over and over, twisting, squirming, writhing, and crumpling up. Now and again one caught a grip on a stanchion or a rope; but the weight of the bodies behind tore such grips loose.

One man I noticed fetched up, head on and square on, with the starboard bitt. His head cracked like an egg. I saw what was coming, sprang on top of the cabin, and from there into the mainsail itself. Ah Choon and one of the Americans tried to follow me, but I was one jump ahead of them. The American was swept away and over the stern like a piece of chaff. Ah Choon caught a spoke of the wheel and swung in behind it. But a strapping Rarotonga *wahine* (woman) — she must have weighed two hundred and fifty — brought up against him and got an arm around his neck. He clutched the Kanaka steersman with his other hand; and just at that moment the schooner flung down to starboard.

The rush of bodies and sea that was coming along the port runway between the captain and the rail turned abruptly and poured to starboard. Away they went — *wahine*, Ah Choon, and steersman; and I swear I saw Ah Choon grin at me with philosophic resignation as he cleared the rail and went under.

The third sea — the biggest of the three — did not do so much damage. By the time it arrived nearly everybody was in the rigging. On deck perhaps a dozen gasping, half-drowned, and half-stunned wretches were rolling about or attempting to crawl into safety. They went by the board, as did the wreckage of the two remaining boats. The other pearl buyers and myself, between seas, managed to get about fifteen women and children into the cabin and battened down. Little good it did the poor creatures in the end.

Wind? Out of all my experience I could not have believed it possible for the wind to blow as it did. There is no describing it. How can one describe a nightmare? It was the same way with that wind. It tore the clothes off our bodies. I say *tore them off*, and I mean it. I am not asking you to believe it. I am merely telling something that I saw and felt. There are times when I do not believe it myself. I went through it, and that is enough. One could not face that wind and live. It was a monstrous thing, and the most monstrous thing about it was that it increased and continued to increase.

Imagine countless millions and billions of tons of sand. Imagine this sand tearing along at ninety, a hundred, a hundred and twenty, or any other number of miles per hour. Imagine, further, this sand to be invisible, impalpable, yet to retain all the weight and density of sand. Do all this, and you may get a vague inkling of what that wind was like.

Perhaps sand is not the right comparison. Consider it mud, invisible, impalpable, but heavy as mud. Nay, it goes beyond that. Consider every molecule of air to be a mudbank in itself. Then try to imagine the multitudinous impact of mudbanks. No; it is beyond me. Language may be adequate to express the ordinary conditions of life, but it cannot possibly express any of the conditions of so enormous a blast of wind. It would have been better had I stuck by my original intention of not attempting a description.

I will say this much: the sea, which had risen at first, was beaten down by that wind. More, it seemed as if the whole ocean had been sucked up in the maw of the hurricane, and hurled on through that portion of space which previously had been occupied by the air.

Of course our canvas had gone long before. But Captain Oudouse had on the *Petite Jeanne* something I had never before seen on a South Sea schooner – a sea anchor. It was a conical canvas bag, the mouth of which was kept open by a huge hoop of iron. The sea anchor was bridled something like a kite, so that it bit into the water as a kite bites into the air, but with a difference. The sea anchor remained just under the surface of the ocean in a perpendicular position. A long line, in turn, connected it with the schooner. As a result the *Petite Jeanne* rode bow on to the wind and to what sea there was.

The situation really would have been favourable had we not been in the path of the storm. True, the wind itself tore our canvas out of the gaskets, jerked out our topmasts, and made a raffle of our running gear, but still we would have come through nicely had we not been square in front of the advancing storm centre. That was what fixed us. I was in a state of stunned, numbed, paralysed collapse from enduring the impact of the wind, and I think I was just about ready to give up and die when the centre smote us. The blow we received was an absolute lull. There was not a breath of air. The effect on one was sickening.

Remember that for hours we had been at terrific muscular tension, withstanding the awful pressure of that wind. And then, suddenly, the pressure was removed. I know that I felt as though I was about to expand, to fly apart in all directions. It seemed as if every atom composing my body was repelling every other atom and was on the verge of rushing off irresistibly into space. But that lasted only for a moment. Destruction was upon us.

In the absence of wind and pressure the sea rose. It jumped, it leaped, it soared straight towards the clouds. Remember, from every point of the compass that inconceivable wind was blowing in towards the centre of calm. The result was that the seas sprang up from every point of the compass. There was no wind to check them. They popped up like corks released from the bottom of a pail of water. There was no system to them, no stability. They were hollow, maniacal seas. They were eighty feet high at the least. They were not seas at all. They resembled no sea a man had ever seen.

They were splashes, monstrous splashes – that is all. Splashes that were eighty feet high. Eighty! They were more than eighty. They went over our mastheads. They were spouts, explosions. They were drunken. They fell anywhere, anyhow. They jostled one another; they collided. They rushed together and collapsed upon one another, or fell apart like a

thousand waterfalls all at once. It was no ocean any man had ever
dreamed of, that hurricane centre. It was confusion thrice confounded. It
was anarchy. It was a hell-pit of sea water gone mad.

The *Petite Jeanne*? I don't know. The heathen told me afterwards that
he did not know. She was literally torn apart, ripped wide open, beaten
into a pulp, smashed into kindling wood, annihilated. When I came to I
was in the water, swimming automatically, though I was about two-thirds
drowned. How I got there I had no recollection. I remembered seeing
the *Petite Jeanne* fly to pieces at what must have been the instant that my
consciousness was buffeted out of me. But there I was, with nothing to
do but make the best of it, and in that best there was little promise. The
wind was blowing again, the sea was much smaller and more regular, and
I knew that I had passed through the centre. Fortunately there were no
sharks about. The hurricane had dissipated the ravenous horde that had
surrounded the death ship and fed off the dead.

It was about midday when the *Petite Jeanne* went to pieces, and it must
have been two hours afterwards that I picked up with one of her hatch
covers. Thick rain was driving at the time; and it was the merest chance
that flung me and the hatch cover together. A short length of line was
trailing from the rope handle; and I knew that I was good for a day, at
least, if the sharks did not return. Three hours later, possibly a little
longer, sticking close to the cover, and with closed eyes concentrating my
whole soul upon the task of breathing in enough air to keep me going
and at the same time of avoiding breathing in enough water to drown
me, it seemed that I heard voices. The rain had ceased, and wind and sea
were easing marvellously. Not twenty feet away from me, on another
hatch cover, were Captain Oudouse and the heathen. They were fighting
over possession of the cover – at least, the Frenchman was.

'*Païen noir!*' I heard him scream, and at the same time I saw him kick
the Kanaka.

Now Captain Oudouse had lost all his clothes except his shoes, and they
were heavy brogans. It was a cruel blow, for it caught the heathen on the
mouth and the point of the chin, half stunning him. I looked for him to
retaliate, but he contented himself with swimming about forlornly a safe ten
feet away. Whenever a fling of the sea threw him closer, the Frenchman,
hanging on with his hands, kicked out at him with both feet. Also, at the
moment of delivering each kick, he called the Kanaka a black heathen.

'For two centimes I'd come over there and drown you, you white
beast!' I yelled.

The only reason I did not go was that I felt too tired. The very
thought of the effort to swim over was nauseating. So I called to the
Kanaka to come to me, and proceeded to share the hatch cover with
him. Otoo, he told me his name was (pronounced ō-t ō-ō); also he told

me that he was a native of Borabora, the most westerly of the Society group. As I learned afterwards, he had got the hatch cover first, and, after some time, encountering Captain Oudouse, had offered to share it with him, and had been kicked off for his pains.

And that was how Otoo and I first came together. He was no fighter. He was all sweetness and gentleness, a love creature, though he stood nearly six feet tall and was muscled like a gladiator. He was no fighter, but he was also no coward. He had the heart of a lion; and in the years that followed I have seen him run risks that I would never dream of taking. What I mean is that while he was no fighter, and while he always avoided precipitating a row, he never ran away from trouble when it started. And it was ''Ware shoal!' when once Otoo went into action. I shall never forget what he did to Bill King. It occurred in German Samoa. Bill King was hailed the champion heavyweight of the American Navy. He was a big brute of a man, a veritable gorilla, one of those hard-hitting, rough-housing chaps, and clever with his fists as well. He picked the quarrel, and he kicked Otoo twice and struck him once before Otoo felt it to be necessary to fight. I don't think it lasted four minutes, at the end of which time Bill King was the unhappy possessor of four broken ribs, a broken forearm, and a dislocated shoulder blade. Otoo knew nothing of scientific boxing. He was merely a manhandler; and Bill King was something like three months in recovering from the bit of manhandling he received that afternoon on Apia beach.

But I am running ahead of my yarn. We shared the hatch cover between us. We took turn and turn about, one lying flat on the cover and resting, while the other, submerged to the neck, merely held on with his hands. For two days and nights, spell and spell, on the cover and in the water, we drifted over the ocean. Towards the last I was delirious most of the time; and there were times, too, when I heard Otoo babbling and raving in his native tongue. Our continuous immersion prevented us from dying of thirst, though the sea water and the sunshine gave us the prettiest imaginable combination of salt-pickle and sunburn.

In the end Otoo saved my life; for I came to lying on the beach twenty feet from the water, sheltered from the sun by a couple of coconut leaves. No one but Otoo could have dragged me there and stuck up the leaves for shade. He was lying beside me. I went off again; and the next time I came round it was cool and starry night, and Otoo was pressing a drinking coconut to my lips.

We were the sole survivors of the *Petite Jeanne*. Captain Oudouse must have succumbed to exhaustion, for several days later his hatch cover drifted ashore without him. Otoo and I lived with the natives of the atoll for about a week, when we were rescued by the French cruiser and taken to Tahiti. In the meantime, however, we had performed the ceremony of exchanging names. In the South Seas such a ceremony binds two men closer together than blood brotherhood. The initiative had been mine; and Otoo was rapturously delighted when I suggested it.

'It is well,' he said in Tahitian. 'For we have been mates together for two days on the lips of Death.'

'But Death stuttered,' I smiled.

'It was a brave deed you did, master,' he replied, 'and Death was not vile enough to speak.'

'Why do you "master" me?' I demanded with a show of hurt feelings. 'We have exchanged names. To you I am Otoo. To me you are Charley. And between you and me, for ever and ever, you shall be Charley, and I shall be Otoo. It is the way of the custom. And when we die, if it does happen that we live again somewhere beyond the stars and the sky, still shall you be Charley to me, and I Otoo to you.'

'Yes, master,' he answered, his eyes luminous and soft with joy.

'There you go!' I cried indignantly.

'What does it matter what my lips utter?' he argued. 'They are only my lips. But I shall think Otoo always. Whenever I think of myself, I shall think of you. Whenever men call me by name, I shall think of you. And beyond the sky and beyond the stars, always and for ever, you shall be Otoo to me. Is it well, master?'

I hid my smile and answered that it was well.

We parted at Papeete. I remained ashore to recuperate; and he went on in a cutter to his own island, Borabora. Six weeks later he was back. I was surprised, for he had told me of his wife, and said that he was returning to her, and would give over sailing on far voyages.

'Where do you go, master?' he asked after our first greetings.

I shrugged my shoulders. It was a hard question.

All the world,' was my answer, 'all the world, all the sea, and all the islands that are in the sea.'

'I will go with you,' he said simply. 'My wife is dead.'

I never had a brother; but from what I have seen of other men's brothers, I doubt if any man ever had a brother that was to him what Otoo was to me. He was brother and father and mother as well. And this I know: I lived a straighter and better man because of Otoo. I cared little for other men, but I had to live straight in Otoo's eyes. Because of him I dared not tarnish myself. He made me his ideal, compounding me, I fear, chiefly out of his own love and worship; and there were times when I stood close to the steep pitch of hell, and would have taken the plunge had not the thought of Otoo restrained me. His pride in me entered into me, until it became one of the major rules in my personal code to do nothing that would diminish that pride of his.

Naturally I did not learn right away what his feelings were towards me.

He never criticized, never censured; and slowly the exalted place I held in his eyes dawned upon me, and slowly I grew to comprehend the hurt I could inflict upon him by being anything less than my best.

For seventeen years we were together; for seventeen years he was at my shoulder, watching while I slept, nursing me through fever and wounds – aye, and receiving wounds in fighting for me. He signed on the same ships with me; and together we ranged the Pacific from Hawaii to Sydney Head, and from Torres Straits to the Galápagos. We blackbirded from the New Hebrides and the Line Islands over to the westward clear through the Louisiades, New Britain, New Ireland, and New Hanover. We were wrecked three times – in the Gilberts, in the Santa Cruz group, and in the Fijis. And we traded and salved wherever a dollar promised in the way of pearl and pearly shell, copra, bêche-de-mer, hawkbill turtle shell, and stranded wrecks.

It began in Papeete, immediately after his announcement that he was going with me all over the sea, and the islands in the midst thereof. There was a club in those days in Papeete, where the pearlers, traders, captains, and riffraff of South Sea adventurers forgathered. The play ran high, and the drink ran high; and I am very much afraid that I kept later hours than were becoming or proper. No matter what the hour was when I left the club, there was Otoo waiting to see me safely home.

At first I smiled; next I chided him. Then I told him flatly that I stood in need of no wet-nursing. After that I did not see him when I came out of the club. Quite by accident, a week or so later, I discovered that he still saw me home, lurking across the street among the shadows of the mango trees. What could I do? I know what I did do.

Insensibly I began to keep better hours. On wet and stormy nights, in the thick of the folly and the fun, the thought would persist in coming to me of Otoo keeping his dreary vigil under the dripping mangoes. Truly, he made a better man of me. Yet he was not strait-laced. And he knew nothing of common Christian morality. All the people on Borabora were Christians; but he was a heathen, the only unbeliever on the island, a gross materialist, who believed that when he died he was dead. He believed merely in fair play and square dealing. Petty meanness, in his code, was almost as serious as wanton homicide; and I do believe that he respected a murderer more than a man given to small practices.

Concerning me, personally, he objected to my doing anything that was hurtful to me. Gambling was all right. He was an ardent gambler himself. But late hours, he explained, were bad for one's health. He had seen men who did not take care of themselves die of fever. He was no teetotaller, and welcomed a stiff nip at any time when it was wet work in the boats. On the other hand, he believed in liquor in moderation. He had seen many men killed or disgraced by squareface or scotch.

Otoo had my welfare always at heart. He thought ahead for me, weighed my plans, and took a greater interest in them than I did myself. At first, when I was unaware of this interest of his in my affairs, he had to divine my intentions, as, for instance, at Papeete, when I contemplated going partners with a knavish fellow-countryman on a guana venture. I did not know he was a knave. Nor did any white man in Papeete. Neither did Otoo know, but he saw how thick we were getting, and found out for me, and without my asking him. Native sailors from the ends of the seas knock about on the beach in Tahiti; and Otoo, suspicious merely, went among them till he had gathered sufficient data to justify his suspicions. Oh, it was a nice history, that of Randolph Waters. I couldn't believe it when Otoo first narrated it; but when I sheeted it home to Waters he gave in without a murmur and got away on the first steamer to Auckland.

At first, I am free to confess, I couldn't help resenting Otoo's poking his nose into my business. But I knew that he was wholly unselfish; and soon I had to acknowledge his wisdom and discretion. He had his eyes open always to my main chance, and he was both keen-sighted and far-sighted. In time he became my counsellor, until he knew more of my business than I did myself. He really had my interest at heart more than I did. Mine was the magnificent carelessness of youth, for I preferred romance to dollars, and adventure to a comfortable billet with all night in. So it was well that I had someone to look out for me. I know that if it had not been for Otoo I should not be here today.

Of numerous instances, let me give one. I had had some experience in blackbirding before I went pearling in the Paumotas. Otoo and I were on the beach in Samoa – we really were on the beach and hard aground – when my chance came to go as recruiter on a blackbird brig. Otoo signed on before the mast; and for the next half-dozen years, in as many ships, we knocked about the wildest portions of Melanesia. Otoo saw to it that he always pulled stroke oar in my boat. Our custom in recruiting labour was to land the recruiter on the beach. The covering boat always lay on its oars several hundred feet offshore, while the recruiter's boat, also lying on its oars, kept afloat on the edge of the beach. While I landed with my trade goods, leaving my steering sweep apeak, Otoo left his stroke position and came into the stern sheets, where a Winchester lay ready to hand under a flap of canvas. The boat's crew was also armed, the Sniders concealed under canvas flaps that ran the length of the gunwales. While I was busy arguing and persuading the woolly-headed cannibals to come and labour on the Queensland plantations, Otoo kept watch. And often and often his low voice warned me of suspicious actions and impending treachery. Sometimes it was the quick shot from his rifle that was the first warning I received. And in my rush to the boat his hand was always there to jerk me flying aboard. Once, I remember, on *Santa Anna*, the boat grounded just as the trouble began. The covering boat was dashing to our assistance, but the several score of savages would have wiped us out before it arrived. Otoo took a flying leap ashore, dug both hands in the trade goods, and scattered tobacco, beads, tomahawks, knives, and calicoes in all directions.

This was too much for the woolly-heads. While they scrambled for the treasures, the boat was shoved clear, and we were aboard and forty feet away. And I got thirty recruits off that very beach in the next four hours.

The particular instance I have in mind was on Malaita, the most savage island in the easterly Solomons. The natives had been remarkably friendly; and how were we to know that the whole village had been taking up a collection for over two years with which to buy a white man's head? The beggars are all head-hunters, and they especially esteem a white man's head. The fellow who captured the head would receive the whole collection. As I say, they appeared very friendly; and on this day I was fully a hundred yards down the beach from the boat. Otoo had cautioned me; and, as usual when I did not heed him, I came to grief.

The first I knew, a cloud of spears sailed out of the mangrove swamp at me. At least a dozen were sticking into me. I started to run, but tripped over one that was fast in my calf, and went down. The woolly-heads made a run for me, each with a long-handled, fantail tomahawk with which to hack off my head. They were so eager for the prize that they got in one another's way. In the confusion I avoided several hacks by throwing myself right and left on the sand.

Then Otoo arrived – Otoo the manhandler. In some way he had got hold of a heavy war club, and at close quarters it was a far more efficient weapon than a rifle. He was right in the thick of them, so that they could not spear him, while their tomahawks seemed worse than useless. He was fighting for me, and he was in a true berserker rage. The way he handled that club was amazing. Their skulls squashed like over-ripe oranges. It was not until he had driven them back, picked me up in his arms, and started to run that he received his first wounds. He arrived in the boat with four spear thrusts, got his Winchester, and with it got a man with every shot. Then we pulled aboard the schooner and doctored up.

Seventeen years we were together. He made me. I should today be a supercargo, a recruiter, or a memory, if it had not been for him.

'You spend your money, and you go out and get more,' he said one day. 'It is easy to get money now. But when you get old, your money will be spent, and you will not be able to go out and get more. I know, master. I have studied the way of white men. On the beaches are many old men who were young once, and who could get money just like you. Now they are old, and they have nothing, and they wait about for the young men like you to come ashore and buy drinks for them.

'The black boy is a slave on the plantation. He gets twenty dollars a year. He works hard. The overseer does not work hard. He rides a horse and watches the black boy work. He gets twelve hundred dollars a year. I am a sailor on the schooner. I get fifteen dollars a month. That is because I am a good sailor. I work hard. The captain has a double awning and drinks beer out of long bottles. I have never seen him haul a rope or pull an oar. He gets one hundred and fifty dollars a month. I am a sailor. He is a navigator. Master, I think it would be very good for you to know navigation.'

Otoo spurred me on to it. He sailed with me as second mate on my first schooner, and he was far prouder of my command than I was myself. Later on it was:

'The captain is well paid, master; but the ship is in his keeping, and he is never free from the burden. It is the owner who is better paid – and the owner who sits ashore with many servants and turns his money over.'

'True, but a schooner costs five thousand dollars – an old schooner at that,' I objected. 'I should be an old man before I saved five thousand dollars.'

'There be short ways for white men to make money,' he went on, pointing ashore at the coconut-fringed beach.

We were in the Solomons at the time, picking up a cargo of ivory nuts along the east coast of Guadalcanal.

'Between this river mouth and the next it is two miles,' he said. 'The flat land runs far back. It is worth nothing now. Next year – who knows? – or the year after, men will pay much money for that land. The anchorage is good. Big steamers can lie close up. You can buy the land four miles deep from the old chief for ten thousand sticks of tobacco, ten bottles of squareface, and a Snider, which will cost you, maybe, one hundred dollars. Then you place the deed with the commissioner; and the next year, or the year after, you sell and become the owner of a ship.'

I followed his lead, and his words came true, though in three years instead of two. Next came the grasslands deal on Guadalcanal – twenty thousand acres, on a governmental nine hundred and ninety-nine years' lease at a nominal sum. I owned the lease for precisely ninety days, when I sold it to a company for half a fortune. Always it was Otoo who looked ahead and saw the opportunity. He was responsible for the salving of the *Doncaster* – bought in at auction for a hundred pounds, and clearing three thousand after every expense was paid. He led me into the Savaii plantation and the cocoa venture on Upolu.

We did not go seafaring so much as in the old days. I was too well off. I married, and my standard of living rose; but Otoo remained the same old-time Otoo, moving about the house or trailing through the office, his wooden pipe in his mouth, a shilling undershirt on his back, and a four-shilling lava-lava about his loins. I could not get him to spend money. There was no way of repaying him except with love, and God knows he got that in full measure from all of us. The children worshipped him and if he had been spoilable, my wife would surely have been his undoing.

The children! He really was the one who showed them the way of their feet in the world practical. He began by teaching them to walk. He sat up with them when they were sick. One by one, when they were scarcely toddlers, he took them down to the lagoon and made them into amphibians. He taught them more than I ever knew of the habits of fish and the ways of catching them. In the bush it was the same thing. At seven Tom knew more woodcraft than I ever dreamed existed. At six Mary went over the Sliding Rock without a quiver, and I had seen strong men balk at that feat. And when Frank had just turned six he could bring up shillings from the bottom in three fathoms.

'My people in Borabora do not like heathen – they are all Christians; and I do not like Borabora Christians,' he said one day, when I, with the idea of getting him to spend some of the money that was rightfully his, had been trying to persuade him to make a visit to his own island in one of our schooners – a special voyage which I had hoped to make a record breaker in the matter of prodigal expense.

I say one of *our* schooners, though legally at the time they belonged to me. I struggled long with him to enter into partnership.

'We have been partners from the day the *Petite Jeanne* went down,' he said at last. 'But if your heart so wishes, then shall we become partners by the law. I have no work to do, yet are my expenses large. I drink and eat and smoke in plenty – it costs much, I know. I do not pay for the playing of billiards, for I play on your table; but still the money goes. Fishing on the reef is only a rich man's pleasure. It is shocking, the cost of hooks and cotton line. Yes; it is necessary that we be partners by law, I need the money. I shall get it from the head clerk in the office.'

So the papers were made out and recorded. A year later I was compelled to complain.

'Charley,' said I, 'you are a wicked old fraud, a miserly skinflint, a miserable land crab. Behold, your share for the year in all our partnerships has been thousands of dollars. The head clerk has given me this paper. It says that in the year you have drawn just eighty-seven dollars and twenty cents.'

'Is there any owing me?' he asked anxiously.

'I tell you thousands and thousands,' I answered.

His face brightened, as with an immense relief.

'It is well,' he said. 'See that the head clerk keeps good account of it. When I want it, I shall want it, and there must not be a cent missing.'

'If there is,' he added fiercely, after a pause, 'it must come out of the clerk's wages.'

And all the time, as I afterwards learned, his will, drawn up by Carruthers, and making me sole beneficiary, lay in the American consul's safe.

But the end came, as the end must come to all human associations. It occurred in the Solomons, where our wildest work had been done in the wild young days, and where we were once more – principally on a holiday, incidentally to look after our holdings on Florida Island and to look over the pearling possibilities of the Mboli Pass. We were lying at Savu, having run in to trade for curios.

Now Savu is alive with sharks. The custom of the woolly-heads of burying their dead in the sea did not tend to discourage the sharks from making the adjacent waters a hangout. It was my luck to be coming aboard in a tiny, overloaded, native canoe when the thing capsized. There were four woolly-heads and myself in it, or, rather hanging to it. The schooner was a hundred yards away. I was just hailing for a boat when one of the woolly-heads began to scream. Holding on to the end of the canoe, both he and that portion of the canoe were dragged under several times. Then he loosed his clutch and disappeared. A shark had got him.

The three remaining woolly-heads tried to climb out of the water upon the bottom of the canoe. I yelled and cursed and struck at the nearest with my fist, but it was no use. They were in a blind funk. The canoe could barely have supported one of them. Under the three it upended and rolled sideways, throwing them back into the water.

I abandoned the canoe and started to swim towards the schooner, expecting to be picked up by the boat before I got there. One of the woolly-heads elected to come with me, and we swam along silently, side by side, now and again putting our faces into the water and peering about for sharks. The screams of the man who stayed by the canoe informed us that he was taken. I was peering into the water when I saw a big shark pass directly beneath me. He was fully sixteen feet in length. I saw the whole thing. He got the woolly-head by the middle, and away he went, the poor devil, head, shoulders, and arms out of water all the time, screeching in a heart-rending way. He was carried along in this fashion for several hundred feet, when he was dragged beneath the surface.

I swam doggedly on, hoping that that was the last unattached shark. But there was another. Whether it was one that had attacked the natives earlier, or whether it was one that had made a good meal elsewhere, I do not know. At any rate, he was not in such haste as the others. I could not swim so rapidly now, for a large part of my effort was devoted to keeping track of him. I was watching him when he made his first attack. By good luck I got both hands on his nose, and though his momentum nearly shoved me under, I managed to keep him off. He veered clear and began circling about again. A second time I escaped him by the same manoeuvre. The third rush was a miss on both sides. He sheered at the moment my hands should have landed on his nose, but his sandpaper hide (I had on a sleeveless undershirt) scraped the skin off one arm from elbow to shoulder.

By this time I was played out, and gave up hope. The schooner was still two hundred feet away. My face was in the water, and I was watching him manoeuvre for another attempt, when I saw a brown body pass between us. It was Otoo.

'Swim for the schooner, master!' he said. And he spoke gaily, as though the affair was a mere lark. 'I know sharks. The shark is my brother.'

I obeyed, swimming slowly on, while Otoo swam about me, keeping always between me and the shark, foiling his rushes and encouraging me.

'The davit tackle carried away, and they are rigging the falls,' he explained a minute or so later, and then went under to head off another attack.

By the time the schooner was thirty feet away I was about done for. I could scarcely move. They were heaving lines at us from on board, but they continually fell short. The shark, finding that it was receiving no hurt, had become bolder. Several times it nearly got me, but each time Otoo was there just the moment before it was too late. Of course Otoo could have saved himself any time. But he stuck by me.

'Good-bye, Charley! I'm finished!' I just managed to gasp.

I knew that the end had come, and that the next moment I should throw up my hands and go down.

But Otoo laughed in my face, saying:

'I will show you a new trick, I will make that shark feel sick!'

He dropped in behind me, where the shark was preparing to come at me.

'A little more to the left!' he next called out. 'There is a line there on the water. To the left, master – to the left!'

I changed my course and struck out blindly. I was by that time barely conscious. As my hands closed on the line I heard an exclamation from on board. I turned and looked. There was no sign of Otoo. The next instant he broke surface. Both hands were off at the wrist, the stumps spouting blood.

'Otoo!' he called softly. And I could see in his gaze the love that thrilled in his voice.

Then, and then only, at the very last of all our years, he called me by that name.

'Good-bye, Otoo!' he called.

Then he was dragged under, and I was hauled aboard, where I fainted in the captain's arms.

And so passed Otoo, who saved me and made me a man, and who saved me in the end. We met in the maw of a hurricane and parted in the maw of a shark, with seventeen intervening years of comradeship, the like of which I dare to assert has never befallen two men, the one brown and the other white. If Jehovah be from His high place watching every sparrow fall, not least in His kingdom shall be Otoo, the one heathen of Borabora.

THE MEXICAN

CHAPTER ONE

Nobody knew his history – they of the Junta least of all. He was their 'little mystery', the 'big patriot', and in his way he worked as hard for the coming Mexican Revolution as did they. They were tardy in recognizing this, for not one of the Junta liked him. The day he first drifted into their crowded, busy rooms they all suspected him of being a spy – one of the bought tools of the Diaz secret service. Too many of the comrades were in civil and military prisons scattered over the United States, and others of them, in irons, were even then being taken across the border to be lined up against adobe walls and shot.

At the first sight the boy did not impress them favourably. Boy he was, not more than eighteen and not over-large for his years. He announced that he was Felipe Rivera, and that it was his wish to work for the revolution. That was all – not a wasted word, no further explanation. He stood waiting. There was no smile on his lips, no geniality in his eyes. Big, dashing Paulino Vera felt an inward shudder. Here was something forbidding, terrible, inscrutable. There was something venomous and snakelike in the boy's black eyes. They burned like cold fire, as with a vast, concentrated bitterness. He flashed them from the faces of the conspirators to the typewriter which little Mrs Sethby was industriously operating. His eyes rested on hers but an instant – she had chanced to look up – and she, too, sensed the nameless something that made her pause. She was compelled to read back in order to regain the swing of the letter she was writing.

Paulino Vera looked questioningly at Arrellano and Ramos, and questioningly they looked back and to each other. The indecision of doubt brooded in their eyes. This slender boy was the Unknown, vested with all the menace of the Unknown. He was unrecognizable, something quite beyond the ken of honest, ordinary revolutionists whose fiercest hatred for Diaz and his tyranny after all was only that of honest and ordinary patriots. Here was something else, they knew not what. But Vera, always the most impulsive, the quickest to act, stepped into the breach.

'Very well,' he said coldly. 'You say you want to work for the

revolution. Take off your coat. Hang it over there. I will show you –
come – where are the buckets and cloths. The floor is dirty. You will
begin by scrubbing it, and by scrubbing the floors of the other rooms.
The spittoons need to be cleaned. Then there are the windows.'

'Is it for the revolution?' the boy asked.

'It is for the revolution,' Vera answered.

Rivera looked cold suspicion at all of them, then proceeded to take off
his coat.

'It is well,' he said.

And nothing more. Day after day he came to his work – sweeping,
scrubbing, cleaning. He emptied the ashes from the stoves, brought up
the coal and kindling, and lighted the fires before the most energetic one
of them was at his desk.

'Can I sleep here?' he asked once.

Aha! So that was it – the hand of Diaz showing through! To sleep in
the rooms of the Junta meant access to their secrets, to the lists of names,
to the addresses of comrades down on Mexican soil. The request was
denied, and Rivera never spoke of it again. He slept they knew not
where, and ate they knew not where or how. Once Arrellano offered
him a couple of dollars. Rivera declined the money with a shake of the
head. When Vera joined in and tried to press it upon him, he said:

'I am working for the revolution.'

It takes money to raise a modern revolution, and always the Junta was
pressed. The members starved and toiled, and the longest day was none
too long, and yet there were times when it appeared as if the revolution
stood or fell on no more than the matter of a few dollars. Once, the first
time, when the rent of the house was two months behind and the
landlord was threatening dispossession, it was Felipe Rivera, the scrub
boy in the poor, cheap clothes, worn and threadbare, who laid sixty
dollars in gold on May Sethby's desk. There were other times. Three
hundred letters, clicked out on the busy typewriters (appeals for
assistance, for sanctions from the organized labour groups, requests for
square news deals to the editors of newspapers, protests against the high-
handed treatment of revolutionists by the United States courts), lay
unmailed, awaiting postage. Vera's watch had disappeared – the old-
fashioned gold repeater that had been his father's. Likewise had gone the
plain gold band from May Sethby's third finger. Things were desperate.
Ramos and Arrellano pulled their long moustaches in despair. The letters
must go off, and the post office allowed no credit to purchasers of stamps.
Then it was that Rivera put on his hat and went out. When he came
back he laid a thousand two-cent stamps on May Sethby's desk.

'I wonder if it is the cursed gold of Diaz?' said Vera to the comrades.

They elevated their brows and could not decide. And Felipe Rivera, the scrubber for the revolution, continued, as occasion arose, to lay down gold and silver for the Junta's use.

And still they could not bring themselves to like him. They did not know him. His ways were not theirs. He gave no confidences. He repelled all probing. Youth that he was, they could never nerve themselves to dare to question him.

'A great and lonely spirit, perhaps. I do not know, I do not know,' Arrellano said helplessly.

'He is not human,' said Ramos.

'His soul has been seared,' said May Sethby. 'Light and laughter have been burned out of him. He is like one dead, and yet he is fearfully alive.'

'He has been through hell,' said Vera. 'No man could look like that who has not been through hell – and he is only a boy.'

Yet they could not like him. He never talked, never inquired, never suggested. He would stand listening, expressionless, a thing dead, save for his eyes, coldly burning, while their talk of the revolution ran high and warm. From face to face and speaker to speaker his eyes would turn, boring like gimlets of incandescent ice, disconcerting and perturbing.

'He is no spy,' Vera confided to May Sethby. 'He is a patriot – mark me, the greatest patriot of us all. I know it, I feel it, here in my heart and head I feel it. But him I know not at all.'

'He has a bad temper,' said May Sethby.

'I know,' said Vera with a shudder. 'He has looked at me with those eyes of his. They do not love; they threaten; they are savage as a wild tiger's. I know, if I should prove unfaithful to the cause, that he would kill me. He has no heart. He is pitiless as steel, keen and cold as frost. He is like moonshine in a winter night when a man freezes to death on some lonely mountain top. I am not afraid of Diaz and all his killers; but this boy, of him am I afraid. I tell you true. I am afraid. He is the breath of death.'

Yet Vera it was who persuaded the others to give the first trust to Rivera. The line of communication between Los Angeles and Lower California had broken down. Three of the comrades had dug their own graves and been shot into them. Two more were United States prisoners in Los Angeles. Juan Alvarado, the federal commander, was a monster. All their plans did he checkmate. They could no longer gain access to the active revolutionists, and the incipient ones, in Lower California.

Young Rivera was given his instructions and dispatched south. When he returned, the line of communication was re-established, and Juan Alvarado was dead. He had been found in bed, a knife hilt-deep in his breast. This had exceeded Rivera's instructions, but they of the Junta knew the times of his movements. They did not ask him. He said nothing. But they looked at one another and conjectured.

'I have told you,' said Vera. 'Diaz has more to fear from this youth than from any man. He is implacable. He is the hand of God.'

The bad temper, mentioned by May Sethby, and sensed by them all, was evidenced by physical proofs. Now he appeared with a cut lip, a blackened cheek, or a swollen ear. It was patent that he brawled, somewhere in that outside world where he ate and slept, gained money, and moved in ways unknown to them. As the time passed he had come to set type for the little revolutionary sheet they published weekly. There were occasions when he was unable to set type, when his knuckles were bruised and battered, when his thumbs were injured and helpless, when one arm or the other hung wearily at his side while his face was drawn with unspoken pain.

'A wastrel,' said Arrellano.

'A frequenter of low places,' said Ramos.

'But where does he get the money?' Vera demanded. 'Only today, just now, have I learned that he paid the bill for white paper – one hundred and forty dollars.'

'There are his absences,' said May Sethby. 'He never explains them.'

'We should set a spy upon him,' Ramos propounded.

'I should not care to be that spy,' said Vera. 'I fear you would never see me again, save to bury me. He has a terrible passion. Not even God would he permit to stand between him and the way of his passion.'

'I feel like a child before him,' Ramos confessed.

'To me he is power – he is the primitive, the wild wolf, the striking rattlesnake, the stinging centipede,' said Arrellano.

'He is the revolution incarnate,' said Vera. 'He is the flame and the spirit of it, the insatiable cry for vengeance that makes no cry but that slays noiselessly. He is a destroying angel moving through the still watches of the night.'

'I could weep over him,' said May Sethby. 'He knows nobody. He hates all people. Us he tolerates, for we are the way of his desire. He is alone . . . lonely.' Her voice broke in a half sob and there was dimness in her eyes.

Rivera's ways and times were truly mysterious. There were periods when they did not see him for a week at a time. Once he was away a month. These occasions were always capped by his return, when, without advertisement or speech, he laid gold coins on May Sethby's desk. Again, for days and weeks, he spent all his time with the Junta. And yet again, for irregular periods, he would disappear through the heart of each day, from early morning until late afternoon. At such times he came early and remained late. Arrellano had found him at midnight, setting type with fresh-swollen knuckles, or mayhap it was his lip, new-split, that still bled.

CHAPTER TWO

The time of the crisis approached. Whether or not the revolution would be depended upon the Junta, and the Junta was hard-pressed. The need for money was greater than ever before, while money was harder to get. Patriots had given their last cent and now could give no more. Section-gang labourers – fugitive peons from Mexico – were contributing half their scanty wages. But more than that was needed. The heartbreaking, conspiring, undermining toil of years approached fruition. The time was ripe. The revolution hung on the balance. One shove more, one last heroic effort, and it would tremble across the scales of victory. They knew their Mexico. Once started, the revolution would take care of itself. The whole Diaz machine would go down like a house of cards. The border was ready to rise. One Yankee, with a hundred I.W.W. men, waited the word to cross over the border and begin the conquest of Lower California. But he needed guns. And clear across to the Atlantic, the Junta in touch with them all and all of them needing guns, mere adventurers, soldiers of fortune, bandits, disgruntled American union men, socialists, anarchists, roughnecks, Mexican exiles, peons escaped from bondage, whipped miners from the bullpens of Coeur d'Alene and Colorado who desired only the more vindictively to fight – all the flotsam and jetsam of wild spirits from the madly complicated modern world. And it was guns and ammunition, ammunition and guns – the unceasing and eternal cry.

Fling this heterogeneous, bankrupt, vindictive mass across the border, and the revolution was on. The custom-house, the northern ports of entry, would be captured. Diaz could not resist. He dared not throw the weight of his armies against them, for he must hold the south. And through the south the flame would spread despite. The people would rise. The defences of city after city would crumple up. State after state would totter down. And at last, from every side, the victorious armies of the revolution would close in on the city of Mexico, itself, Diaz's last stronghold.

But the money. They had the men, impatient and urgent, who would use the guns. They knew the traders who would sell and deliver the guns. But to culture the revolution thus far had exhausted the Junta. The last dollar had been spent, the last resource and the last starving patriot milked dry, and the great adventure still trembled on the scales. Guns and ammunition! The ragged battalions must be armed. But how? Ramos lamented his confiscated estates. Arrellano wailed the spendthriftness of his youth. May Sethby wondered if it would have been different had they of the Junta been more economical in the past.

'To think that the freedom of Mexico should stand or fall on a few paltry thousands of dollars,' said Paulino Vera.

Despair was in all their faces. José Amarillo, their last hope, a recent convert who had promised money, had been apprehended at his hacienda in Chihuahua and shot against his own stable wall. The news had just come through.

Rivera, on his knees, scrubbing, looked up, with suspended brush, his bare arms flecked with soapy, dirty water.

'Will five thousand do it?' he asked.

They looked their amazement. Vera nodded and swallowed. He could not speak, but he was on the instant invested with a vast faith.

'Order the guns,' Rivera said, and thereupon was guilty of the longest flow of words they had ever heard him utter. 'The time is short. In three weeks I shall bring you the five thousand. It is well. The weather will be warmer for those who fight. Also, it is the best I can do.'

Vera fought his faith. It was incredible. Too many fond hopes had been shattered since he had begun to play the revolution game. He believed this threadbare scrubber of the revolution, and yet he dared not believe.

'You are crazy,' he said.

'In three weeks,' said Rivera. 'Order the guns.'

He got up, rolled down his sleeves, and put on his coat.

'Order the guns,' he said. 'I am going now.'

CHAPTER THREE

After hurrying and scurrying, much telephoning and bad language, a night session was held in Kelly's office. Kelly was rushed with business; also, he was unlucky. He had brought Danny Ward out from New York, arranged the fight for him with Billy Carthey, the date was three weeks away, and for two days now, carefully concealed from the sporting writers, Carthey had been lying up, badly injured. There was no one to take his place. Kelly had been burning the wires east to every eligible lightweight, but they were tied up with dates and contracts. And now hope had revived, though faintly.

'You've got a hell of a nerve,' Kelly addressed Rivera, after one look, as soon as they got together.

Hate that was malignant was in Rivera's eyes, but his face remained impassive.

'I can lick Ward,' was all he said.

'How do you know? Ever see him fight?'

Rivera shook his head.

'He can beat you up with one hand and both eyes closed.'

Rivera shrugged his shoulders.

'Haven't you got anything to say?' the fight promoter snarled.

'I can lick him.'

'Who'd you ever fight, anyway?' Michael Kelly demanded. Michael was the promoter's brother, and ran the Yellowstone Poolrooms, where he made goodly sums on the fight game.

Rivera favoured him with a bitter, unanswering stare.

The promoter's secretary, a distinctively sporty young man, sneered audibly.

'Well, you know Roberts,' Kelly broke the hostile silence. 'He ought to be here. I've sent for him. Sit down and wait, though from the looks of you, you haven't got a chance. I can't throw the public down with a bum fight. Ringside seats are selling at fifteen dollars, you know that.'

When Roberts arrived it was patent that he was mildly drunk. He was a tall, lean, slack-jointed individual, and his walk, like his talk, was a smooth and languid drawl.

Kelly went straight to the point.

'Look here, Roberts, you've been braggin' you discovered this little Mexican. You know Carthey's broken his arm. Well, this little yellow streak has the gall to blow in today and say he'll take Carthey's place. What about it?'

'It's all right, Kelly,' came the slow response. 'He can put up a fight.'

'I suppose you'll be sayin' next that he can lick Ward,' Kelly snapped.

Roberts considered judicially.

'No, I won't say that. Ward's a topnotcher and a ring general. But he can't hash-house Rivera in short order. I know Rivera. Nobody can get his goat. He ain't got a goat that I could ever discover. And he's a two-handed fighter. He can throw in the sleep-makers from any position.'

'Never mind that. What kind of a show can he put up? You've been conditioning and training fighters all your life. I take off my hat to your judgment. Can he give the public a run for its money?'

'He sure can, and he'll worry Ward a mighty heap on top of it. You don't know that boy. I do. I discovered him. He ain't got a goat. He's a devil. He's a wizzy-wooz if anybody should ask you. He'll make Ward sit up with a show of local talent that'll make the rest of you sit up. I won't say he'll lick Ward, but he'll put up such a show that you'll all know he's a comer.'

'All right.' Kelly turned to his secretary. 'Ring up Ward. I warned him to show up if I thought it worth while. He's right across at the Yellowstone, throwin' chests and doing the popular.' Kelly turned back to the conditioner. 'Have a drink?'

Roberts sipped his highball and unburdened himself.

'Never told you how I discovered the little cuss. It was a couple of years ago he showed up out at the quarters. I was getting Prayne ready

for his fight with Delaney. Prayne's wicked. He ain't got a tickle of mercy
in his make-up. He'd chopped up his pardners something cruel, and I
couldn't find a willing boy that'd work with him. I'd noticed this little
starved Mexican kid hanging around, and I was desperate. So I grabbed
him, slammed on the gloves, and put him in. He was tougher'n rawhide,
but weak. And he didn't know the first letter in the alphabet of boxing.
Prayne chopped him to ribbons. But he hung on for two sickening
rounds, when he fainted. Starvation, that was all. Battered? You couldn't
have recognized him. I gave him half a dollar and a square meal. You
oughta seen him wolf it down. He hadn't had a bite for a couple of days.
That's the end of him, thinks I. But next day he showed up, stiff an' sore,
ready for another half and a square meal. And he done better as time
went by. Just a born fighter, and tough beyond belief. He hasn't a heart.
He's a piece of ice. And he never talked eleven words in a string since I
know him. He saws wood and does his work.'

'I've seen 'm,' the secretary said. 'He's worked a lot for you.'

'All the big little fellows has tried out on him,' Roberts answered. 'And
he's learned from 'em. I've seen some of them he could lick. But his
heart wasn't in it. I reckoned he never liked the game. He seemed to act
that way.'

'He's been fighting some before the little clubs the last few months,'
Kelly said.

'Sure. But I don't know what struck 'm. All of a sudden his heart got into
it. He just went out like a streak and cleaned up all the little local fellows.
Seemed to want the money, and he's won a bit, though his clothes don't
look it. He's peculiar. Nobody knows his business. Nobody knows how he
spends his time. Even when he's on the job, he plumb up and disappears
most of each day soon as his work is done. Sometimes he just blows away
for weeks at a time. But he don't take advice. There's a fortune in it for the
fellow that gets the job of managin' him, only he won't consider it. And
you watch him hold out for the cash money when you get down to terms.'

It was at this stage that Danny Ward arrived. Quite a party it was. His
manager and trainer were with him, and he breezed in like a gusty
draught of geniality, good nature, and all-conqueringness. Greetings flew
about, a joke here, a retort there, a smile or a laugh for everybody. Yet it
was his way, and only partly sincere. He was a good actor, and he had
found geniality a most valuable asset in the game of getting on in the
world. But down underneath he was the deliberate, cold-blooded fighter
and businessman. The rest was a mask. Those who knew him or
trafficked with him said that when it came to brass tacks he was Danny
on the Spot. He was invariably present at all business discussions, and it
was urged by some that his manager was a blind whose only function was
to serve as Danny's mouthpiece.

Rivera's way was different. Indian blood, as well as Spanish, was in his veins, and he sat back in a corner, silent, immobile, only his black eyes passing from face to face and noting everything.

'So that's the guy,' Danny said, running an appraising eye over his proposed antagonist. 'How de do, old chap?'

Rivera's eyes burned venomously, but he made no sign of acknowledgment. He disliked all gringos, but this gringo he hated with an immediacy that was unusual even in him.

'Gawd!' Danny protested facetiously to the promoter. 'You ain't expectin' me to fight a deaf mute.' When the laughter subsided he made another hit. 'Los Angeles must be on the dink when this is the best you can scare up. What kindergarten did you get 'm from?'

'He's a good little boy, Danny, take it from me,' Roberts defended. 'Not as easy as he looks.'

'And half the house is sold already,' Kelly pleaded. 'You'll have to take 'm on, Danny. It's the best we can do.'

Danny ran another careless and unflattering glance over Rivera and sighed.

'I gotta be easy with 'm, I guess. If only he don't blow up.'

Roberts snorted.

'You gotta be careful,' Danny's manager warned. 'No taking chances with a dub that's likely to sneak a lucky one across.'

'Oh, I'll be careful all right, all right,' Danny smiled. 'I'll get 'm at the start an' nurse 'm along for the dear public's sake. What d'ye say to fifteen rounds, Kelly – an' then the hay for him?'

'That'll do,' was the answer. 'As long as you make it realistic.'

'Then let's get down to biz.' Danny paused and calculated. 'Of course, sixty-five per cent of gate receipts, same as with Carthey. But the split'll be different. Eighty will just about suit me.' And to his manager, 'That right?'

The manager nodded.

'Here, you, did you get that?' Kelly asked Rivera.

Rivera shook his head.

'Well, it's this way,' Kelly exposited. 'The purse'll be sixty-five per cent of the gate receipts. You're a dub, and an unknown. You and Danny split, twenty per cent goin' to you, an' eighty to Danny. That's fair, isn't it, Roberts?'

'Very fair,' Roberts agreed. 'You see, you ain't got a reputation yet.'

'What will sixty-five per cent of the gate receipts be?' Rivera demanded.

'Oh, maybe five thousand, maybe as high as eight thousand,' Danny broke in to explain. 'Something like that. Your share'll come to something like a thousand or sixteen hundred. Pretty good for takin' a licking from a guy with my reputation. What d'ye say?'

Then Rivera took their breaths away.

'Winner takes all,' he said with finality.

A dead silence prevailed.

'It's like candy from a baby,' Danny's manager proclaimed.

Danny shook his head.

'I've been in the game too long,' he explained. 'I'm not casting reflections on the referee or the present company. I'm not sayin' nothing about bookmakers an' frame-ups that sometimes happen. But what I do say is that it's poor business for a fighter like me. I play safe. There's no tellin'. Mebbe I break my arm, eh? Or some guy slips me a bunch of dope.' He shook his head solemnly. 'Win or lose, eighty is my split. What d'ye say, Mexican?'

Rivera shook his head.

Danny exploded. He was getting down to brass tacks now.

'Why, you dirty little greaser! I've a mind to knock your block off right now.'

Roberts drawled his body to interposition between hostilities.

'Winner takes all,' Rivera repeated sullenly.

'Why do you stand out that way?' Danny asked.

'I can lick you,' was the straight answer.

Danny half started to take off his coat. But, as his manager knew, it was grandstand play. The coat did not come off, and Danny allowed himself to be placated by the group. Everybody sympathized with him. Rivera stood alone.

'Look here, you little fool,' Kelly took up the argument. 'You're nobody. We know what you've been doing the last few months – putting away little local fighters. But Danny is class. His next fight after this will be for the championship. And you're unknown. Nobody ever heard of you out of Los Angeles.'

'They will,' Rivera answered with a shrug, 'after this fight.'

'You think for a second you can lick me?' Danny blurted in.

Rivera nodded.

'Oh, come; listen to reason,' Kelly pleaded. 'Think of the advertising.'

'I want the money,' was Rivera's answer.

'You couldn't win from me in a thousand years,' Danny assured him.

'Then what are you holding out for?' Rivera countered. 'If the money's that easy, why don't you go after it?'

'I will, so help me!' Danny cried with abrupt conviction. 'I'll beat you to death in the ring, my boy – you monkeyin' with me this way. Make out the articles, Kelly. Winner take all. Play it up in the sportin' columns. Tell 'em it's a grudge fight. I'll show this fresh kid a few.'

Kelly's secretary had begun to write, when Danny interrupted.

'Hold on!' He turned to Rivera. 'Weights?'

'Ringside,' came the answer.

'Not on your life, fresh kid. If winner takes all, we weigh in at 10 a.m.'

'And winner takes all?' Rivera queried.

Danny nodded. That settled it. He would enter the ring in his full ripeness of strength.

'Weigh in at ten,' Rivera said.

The secretary's pen went on scratching.

'It means five pounds,' Roberts complained to Rivera. 'You've given too much away. You've thrown the fight right there. Danny'll be as strong as a bull. You're a fool. He'll lick you sure. You ain't got the chance of a dewdrop in hell.'

Rivera's answer was a calculated look of hatred. Even this gringo he despised, and him had he found the whitest gringo of them all.

CHAPTER FOUR

Barely noticed was Rivera as he entered the ring. Only a very slight and very scattering ripple of half-hearted hand-clapping greeted him. The house did not believe in him. He was the lamb led to slaughter at the hands of the great Danny. Besides, the house was disappointed. It had expected a rushing battle between Danny Ward and Billy Carthey, and here it must put up with this poor little tyro. Still further, it had manifested its disapproval of the change of betting two, and even three, to one on Danny. And where a betting audience's money is, there is its heart.

The Mexican boy sat down in his corner and waited. The slow minutes lagged by. Danny was making him wait. It was an old trick, but ever it worked on the young, new fighters. They grew frightened, sitting thus and facing their own apprehensions and a callous, tobacco-smoking audience. But for once the trick failed. Roberts was right. Rivera had no goat. He, who was more delicately co-ordinated, more finely nerved and strung than any of them, had no nerves of this sort. The atmosphere of foredoomed defeat in his own corner had no effect on him. His handlers were gringos and strangers. Also they were scrubs – the dirty driftage of the fight game, without honour, without efficiency. And they were chilled, as well, with certitude that theirs was the losing corner.

'Now you gotta be careful,' Spider Hagerty warned him. Spider was his chief second. 'Make it last as long as you can – them's my instructions from Kelly. If you don't, the papers'll call it another bum fight and give the game a bigger black eye in Los Angeles.'

All of which was not encouraging. But Rivera took no notice. He despised prize fighting. It was the hated game of the hated gringo. He had taken up with it, as a chopping block for others in the training quarters, solely because he was starving. The fact that he was marvellously made for it had meant nothing. He hated it. Not until he had come in to the Junta had he fought for money, and he had found the money easy. Not first among the sons of men had he been to find himself successful at a despised vocation.

He did not analyse. He merely knew that he must win this fight. There could be no other outcome. For behind him, nerving him to this belief, were profounder forces than any the crowded house dreamed. Danny Ward fought for money and for the easy ways of life that money would bring. But the things Rivera fought for burned in his brain – blazing and terrible visions, that, with eyes wide open, sitting lonely in the corner of the ring and waiting for his tricky antagonist, he saw as clearly as he had lived them.

He saw the white-walled, water-power factories of Rio Blanco. He saw the six thousand workers, starved and wan, and the little children, seven and eight years of age, who toiled long shifts for ten cents a day. He saw the perambulating corpses, the ghastly death's heads of men who laboured in the dye rooms. He remembered that he had heard his father call the dye rooms the 'suicide holes', where a year was death. He saw the little patio, and his mother cooking and moiling at crude housekeeping and finding time to caress and love him. And his father he saw, large, big-moustached, and deep-chested, kindly above all men, who loved all men and whose heart was so large that there was love to overflowing still left for the mother and the little *muchacho* playing in the corner of the patio. In those days his name had not been Felipe Rivera. It had been Fernandez, his father's and mother's name. Him had they called Juan. Later he had changed it himself, for he had found the name of Fernandez hated by prefects of police, *jefes politicos*, and *rurales*.

Big, hearty Joaquin Fernandez! A large place he occupied in Rivera's visions. He had not understood at the time, but, looking back, he could understand. He could see him setting type in the little printery, or scribbling endless hasty, nervous lines on the much-cluttered desk. And he could see the strange evenings, when workmen, coming secretly in the dark like men who did ill deeds, met with his father and talked long hours where he, the muchacho, lay not always asleep in the corner.

As from a remote distance he could hear Spider Hagerty saying to him: 'No layin' down at the start. Them's instructions. Take a beatin' an' earn your dough.'

Ten minutes had passed, and he still sat in his corner. There were no signs of Danny, who was evidently playing the trick to the limit.

But more visions burned before the eye of Rivera's memory. The strike, or, rather, the lock-out, because the workers of Rio Blanco had helped their striking brothers of Puebla. The hunger, the expeditions in the hills for berries, the roots and herbs that all ate and that twisted and pained the stomachs of all of them. And then the nightmare; the waste of ground before the company's store; the thousands of starving workers; General Rosalio Martinez and the soldiers of Porfirio Diaz; and the death-spitting rifles that seemed never to cease spitting, while the workers' wrongs were washed and washed again in their own blood. And that night! He saw the flat cars, piled high with the bodies of the slain, consigned to Vera Cruz, food for the sharks of the bay. Again he crawled over the grisly heaps, seeking and finding, stripped and mangled his father and mother. His mother he especially remembered – only her face projecting, her body burdened by the weight of dozens of bodies. Again the rifles of the soldiers of Porfirio Diaz cracked, and again he dropped to the ground and slunk away like some hunted coyote of the hills.

To his ears came a great roar, as of the sea, and he saw Danny Ward, leading his retinue of trainers and seconds, coming down the centre aisle. The house was in wild uproar for the popular hero who was bound to win. Everybody proclaimed him. Everybody was for him. Even Rivera's own seconds warmed to something akin to cheerfulness when Danny ducked jauntily through the ropes and entered the ring. His face continually spread to an unending succession of smiles, and when Danny smiled he smiled in every feature, even to the laughter wrinkles of the corners of the eyes and into the depths of the eyes themselves. Never was there so genial a fighter. His face was a running advertisement of good feeling, of good-fellowship. He knew everybody. He joked, and laughed, and greeted his friends through the ropes. Those farther away, unable to suppress their admiration, cried loudly: 'Oh, you Danny!' It was a joyous ovation of affection that lasted a full five minutes.

Rivera was disregarded. For all that the audience noticed, he did not exist. Spider Hagerty's bloated face bent down close to his.

'No gettin' scared,' the Spider warned. 'An' remember instructions. You gotta last. No layin' down. If you lay down, we got instructions to beat you up in the dressing-rooms. Savvy? You just gotta fight.'

The house began to applaud. Danny was crossing the ring to him. Danny bent over him, caught Rivera's right hand in both his own and shook it with impulsive heartiness. Danny's smile-wreathed face was close to his. The audience yelled its appreciation of Danny's display of sporting spirit. He was greeting his opponent with the fondness of a brother. Danny's lips moved, and the audience, interpreting the unheard words to be those of a kindly-natured sport, yelled again. Only Rivera heard the low words.

'You little Mexican rat,' hissed from between Danny's gaily smiling lips, 'I'll fetch the yellow outa you.'

Rivera made no move. He did not rise. He merely hated with his eyes.

'Get up, you dog!' some man yelled through the ropes from behind.

The crowd began to hiss and boo him for his unsportsmanlike conduct, but he sat unmoved. Another great outburst of applause was Danny's as he walked back across the ring.

When Danny stripped, there were ohs! and ahs! of delight. His body was perfect, alive with easy suppleness and health and strength. The skin was white as a woman's, and as smooth. All grace, and resilience, and power resided therein. He had proved it in scores of battles. His photographs were in all the physical-culture magazines.

A groan went up as Spider Hagerty peeled Rivera's sweater over his head. His body seemed leaner because of the swarthiness of the skin. He had muscles, but they made no display like his opponent's. What the audience neglected to see was the deep chest. Nor could it guess the toughness of the fibre of the flesh, the instantaneousness of the cell explosions of the muscles, the fineness of the nerves that wired every part of him into a splendid fighting mechanism. All the audience saw was a brown-skinned boy of eighteen with what seemed the body of a boy. With Danny it was different. Danny was a man of twenty-four, and his body was a man's body. The contrast was still more striking as they stood together in the centre of the ring receiving the referee's last instructions.

Rivera noticed Roberts sitting directly behind the newspapermen. He was drunker than usual, and his speech was correspondingly slower.

'Take it easy, Rivera,' Roberts drawled. 'He can't kill you, remember that. He'll rush you at the go-off, but don't get rattled. You just cover up, and stall, and clinch. He can't hurt you much. Just make believe to yourself that he's choppin' out on you at the trainin' quarters.'

Rivera made no sign that he had heard.

'Sullen little devil,' Roberts muttered to the man next to him. 'He always was that way.'

But Rivera forgot to look his usual hatred. A vision of countless rifles blinded his eyes. Every face in the audience, as far as he could see, to the high dollar seats, was transformed into a rifle. And he saw the long Mexican border arid and sun-washed and aching, and along it he saw the ragged bands that delayed only for the guns.

Back in his corner he waited, standing up. His seconds had crawled out through the ropes, taking the canvas stool with them. Diagonally across the squared ring, Danny faced him. The gong struck, and the battle was on. The audience howled its delight. Never had it seen a battle open more convincingly. The papers were right. It was a grudge fight. Three-quarters of the distance Danny covered in the rush to get together, his intention to eat up the Mexican lad plainly advertised. He assailed with not one blow, nor two, nor a dozen. He was a gyroscope of blows, a whirlwind of destruction. Rivera was nowhere. He was overwhelmed, buried beneath avalanches of punches delivered from every angle and position by a past master in the art. He was overborne, swept back against the ropes, separated by the referee, and swept back against the ropes again.

It was not a fight. It was a slaughter, a massacre. Any audience, save a prize-fighting one, would have exhausted its emotions in that first minute. Danny was certainly showing what he could do – a splendid exhibition. Such was the certainty of the audience, as well as its excitement and favouritism, that it failed to notice that the Mexican still stayed on his feet. It forgot Rivera. It rarely saw him, so closely was he enveloped in Danny's man-eating attack. A minute of this went by, and two minutes. Then, in a separation, it caught a clear glimpse of the Mexican. His lip was cut, his nose was bleeding. As he turned and staggered into a clinch the welts of oozing blood, from his contacts with the ropes, showed in red bars across his back. But what the audience did not notice was that his chest was not heaving and that his eyes were coldly burning as ever. Too many aspiring champions, in the cruel welter of the training camps, had practised this man-eating attack on him. He had learned to live through for a compensation of from half a dollar a go up to fifteen dollars a week – a hard school, and he was schooled hard.

Then happened the amazing thing. The whirling, blurring mix-up ceased suddenly. Rivera stood alone. Danny, the redoubtable Danny, lay on his back. His body quivered as consciousness strove to return to it. He had not staggered and sunk down, nor had he gone over in a long slumping fall. The right hook of Rivera had dropped him in mid-air with the abruptness of death. The referee shoved Rivera back with one hand and stood over the fallen gladiator counting the seconds. It is the custom of prize-fighting audiences to cheer a clean knock-down blow. But this audience did not cheer. The thing had been too unexpected. It watched the toll of the seconds in tense silence, and through this silence the voice of Roberts rose exultantly:

'I told you he was a two-handed fighter!'

By the fifth second Danny was rolling on his face, and when seven was counted he rested on one knee, ready to rise after the count of nine and before the count of ten. If his knee still touched the floor at 'ten' he was considered 'down' and also 'out'. The instant his knee left the floor he was considered 'up', and in that instant it was Rivera's right to try and put him down again. Rivera took no chances. The moment that knee left the floor he would strike again. He circled around, but the referee circled in between, and Rivera knew that the seconds he counted were very slow. All gringos were against him, even the referee.

At 'nine' the referee gave Rivera a sharp thrust back. It was unfair, but it enabled Danny to rise, the smile back on his lips. Doubled partly over, with arms wrapped about face and abdomen, he cleverly stumbled into a clinch. By all the rules of the game the referee should have broken it, but he did not, and Danny clung on like a surf-battered barnacle and moment by moment recuperated. The last minute of the round was going fast. If he could live to the end he would have a full-minute in his corner to revive. And live to the end he did, smiling through all desperateness and extremity.

'The smile that won't come off!' somebody yelled, and the audience laughed loudly in its relief.

'The kick that greaser's got is something God-awful,' Danny gasped in his corner to his adviser while his handlers worked frantically over him.

The second and third rounds were tame. Danny, a tricky and consummate ring general, stalled and blocked and held on, devoting himself to recovering from that dazing, first-round blow. In the fourth round he was himself again. Jarred and shaken, nevertheless his good condition had enabled him to regain his vigour. But he tried no man-eating tactics. The Mexican had proved a tartar. Instead he brought to bear his best fighting powers. In tricks and skill and experience he was the master, and though he could land nothing vital, he proceeded scientifically to chop and wear down his opponent. He landed three blows to Rivera's one, but they were punishing blows only, and not deadly. It was the sum of many of them that constituted deadliness. He was respectful of this two-handed dub with the amazing short-arm kicks in both his fists.

In defence Rivera developed a disconcerting straight left. Again and again, attack after attack he straight-lefted away from him with accumulated damage to Danny's mouth and nose. But Danny was protean. That was why he was the coming champion. He could change from style to style of fighting at will. He now devoted himself to infighting. In this he was particularly wicked, and it enabled him to avoid the other's straight left. Here he set the house wild repeatedly, capping it with a marvellous lock-break and lift of an inside uppercut that raised the Mexican in the air and dropped him to the mat. Rivera rested on one knee, making the most of the count, and in the soul of him knew the referee was counting short seconds on him.

Again, in the seventh, Danny achieved the diabolical inside uppercut. He succeeded only in staggering Rivera, but in the ensuing moment of defenceless helplessness he smashed him with another blow through the ropes. Rivera's body bounced on the heads of the newspapermen below, and they boosted him back to the edge of the platform outside the ropes. Here he rested on one knee, while the referee raced off the seconds. Inside the ropes, through which he must duck to enter the ring, Danny waited for him. Nor did the referee intervene or thrust Danny back.

The house was beside itself with delight.

'Kill 'm, Danny, kill 'm!' was the cry.

Scores of voices took it up until it was like a war chant of wolves.

Danny did his best, but Rivera, at the count of eight, instead of nine, came unexpectedly through the ropes and safely into a clinch. Now the referee worked, tearing him away so that he could be hit, giving Danny every advantage that an unfair referee can give.

But Rivera lived, and the daze cleared from his brain. It was all of a piece. They were the hated gringos and they were unfair. And in the worst of it visions continued to flash and sparkle in his brain – long lines of railroad track that simmered across the desert; *rurales* and American constables; prisons and calabooses; tramps at water tanks – all the squalid and painful panorama of his odyssey after Rio Blanco and the strike. And, resplendent and glorious, he saw the great red revolution sweeping across his land. The guns were there before him. Every hated face was a gun. It was for the guns he fought. He was the guns. He was the revolution. He fought for all Mexico.

The audience began to grow incensed with Rivera. Why didn't he take the licking that was appointed him? Of course he was going to be licked, but why should he be so obstinate about it? Very few were interested in him, and they were the certain, definite percentage of a gambling crowd that plays long shots. Believing Danny to be the winner, nevertheless they had put their money on the Mexican at four to ten and one to three. More than a trifle was up on the point of how many rounds Rivera could last. Wild money had appeared at the ringside proclaiming that he could not last seven rounds, or even six. The winners of this, now that their cash risk was happily settled, had joined in cheering on the favourite.

Rivera refused to be licked. Through the eighth round his opponent strove vainly to repeat the uppercut. In the ninth Rivera stunned the house again. In the midst of a clinch he broke the lock with a quick, lithe movement, and in the narrow space between their bodies his right lifted from the waist. Danny went to the floor and took the safety of the count. The crowd was appalled. He was being bested at his own game. His famous right uppercut had been worked back on him. Rivera made no attempt to catch him as he arose at 'nine'. The referee was openly blocking that play, though he stood clear when the situation was reversed and it was Rivera who required to rise.

Twice in the tenth Rivera put through the right uppercut, lifted from waist to opponent's chin. Danny grew desperate. The smile never left his face, but he went back to his man-eating rushes. Whirlwind as he would, he could not damage Rivera, while Rivera, through the blur and whirl, dropped him to the mat three times in succession. Danny did not recuperate so quickly now, and by the eleventh round he was in a serious way. But from then till the fourteenth he put up the gamest exhibition of his career. He stalled and blocked, fought parsimoniously, and strove to gather strength. Also he fought as foully as a successful fighter knows how. Every trick and device he employed, butting in the clinches with the seeming of accident, pinioning Rivera's glove between arm and body, heeling his glove on Rivera's mouth to clog his breathing. Often, in the clinches, through his cut and smiling lips he snarled insults unspeakable and vile in Rivera's ear. Everybody, from the referee to the house, was with Danny and was helping Danny. And they knew what he had in mind. Bested by this surprise box of an unknown, he was pinning all on a single punch. He offered himself for punishment, fished, and feinted, and drew, for that one opening that would enable him to whip a blow through with all his strength and turn the tide. As another and greater fighter had done before him, he might do – a right and left, to solar plexus and across the jaw. He could do it, for he was noted for the strength of punch that remained in his arms as long as he could keep his feet.

Rivera's seconds were not half caring for him in the intervals between rounds. Their towels made a showing but drove little air into his panting lungs. Spider Hagerty talked advice to him, but Rivera knew it was wrong advice. Everybody was against him. He was surrounded by treachery. In the fourteenth round he put Danny down again, and himself stood resting, hands dropped at side, while the referee counted. In the other corner Rivera had been noting suspicious whisperings. He saw Michael Kelly make his way to Roberts and bend and whisper. Rivera's ears were a cat's, desert-trained, and he caught snatches of what was said. He wanted to hear more, and when his opponent arose he manoeuvred the fight into a clinch over against the ropes.

'Got to,' he could hear Michael, while Roberts nodded. 'Danny's got to win – I stand to lose a mint. I've got a ton of money covered – my own. If he lasts the fifteenth I'm bust. The boy'll mind you. Put something across.'

And thereafter Rivera saw no more visions. They were trying to job him. Once again he dropped Danny and stood resting, his hands at his side. Roberts stood up.

'That settled him,' he said. 'Go to your corner.'

He spoke with authority, as he had often spoken to Rivera at the training quarters. But Rivera looked hatred at him and waited for Danny to rise. Back in his corner in the minute interval, Kelly, the promoter, came and talked to Rivera.

'Throw it, damn you,' he rasped in a harsh low voice. 'You gotta lay down, Rivera. Stick with me and I'll make your future. I'll let you lick

Danny next time. But here's where you lay down.'

Rivera showed with his eyes that he heard, but he made neither sign of assent nor dissent.

'Why don't you speak?' Kelly demanded angrily.

'You lose anyway,' Spider Hagerty supplemented. 'The referee'll take it away from you. Listen to Kelly and lay down.'

'Lay down, kid,' Kelly pleaded, 'and I'll help you to the championship.'

Rivera did not answer.

'I will, so help me, kid.'

At the strike of the gong Rivera sensed something impending. The house did not. Whatever it was, it was there inside the ring with him and very close. Danny's early surety seemed returned to him. The confidence of his advance frightened Rivera. Some trick was about to be worked. Danny rushed, but Rivera refused the encounter. He side-stepped away into safety. What the other wanted was a clinch. It was in some way necessary to the trick. Rivera backed and circled away, yet he knew, sooner or later, the clinch and the trick would come. Desperately he resolved to draw it. He made as if to effect the clinch with Danny's next rush. Instead, at the last instant, just as their bodies should have come together, Rivera darted nimbly back. And in the same instant Danny's corner raised a cry of foul. Rivera had fooled them. The referee paused irresolutely. The decision that trembled on his lips was never uttered, for a shrill, boy's voice from the gallery piped, 'Raw work!'

Danny cursed Rivera openly, and forced him, while Rivera danced away. Also Rivera made up his mind to strike no more blows at the body. In this he threw away half his chance of winning, but he knew if he was to win at all it was with the outfighting that remained to him. Given the least opportunity, they would lie a foul on him. Danny threw all caution to the winds. For two rounds he tore after and into the boy who dared not meet him at close quarters. Rivera was struck again and again; he took blows by the dozens to avoid the perilous clinch. During this supreme final of Danny's the audience rose to its feet and went mad. It did not understand. All it could see was that its favourite was winning after all.

'Why don't you fight?' it demanded wrathfully of Rivera. 'You're yellow! You're yellow!' 'Open up, you cur! Open up!' 'Kill 'm, Danny! Kill 'm!' 'You sure got 'm! Kill 'm!'

In all the house, bar none, Rivera was the only cold man. By temperament and blood he was the hottest-passioned there; but he had gone through such vastly greater heats that this collective passion of ten thousand throats, rising surge on surge, was to his brain no more than the velvet cool of a summer twilight.

Into the seventeenth round Danny carried his rally. Rivera, under a heavy blow, drooped and sagged. His hands dropped helplessly as he reeled backwards. Danny thought it was his chance. The boy was at his mercy. Thus Rivera, feigning, caught him off his guard, lashing out a clean drive to the mouth. Danny went down. When he arose Rivera felled him with a down-chop of the right on neck and jaw. Three times he repeated this. It was impossible for any referee to call these blows foul.

'Oh, Bill! Bill!' Kelly pleaded to the referee.

'I can't,' that official lamented back. 'He won't give me a chance.'

Danny, battered and heroic, still kept coming up. Kelly and others near to the ring began to cry out to the police to stop it, though Danny's corner refused to throw in the towel. Rivera saw the fat police captain starting awkwardly to climb through the ropes, and was not sure what it meant. There were so many ways of cheating in this game of the gringos. Danny, on his feet, tottered groggily and helplessly before him. The referee and the captain were both reaching for Rivera when he struck the last blow. There was no need to stop the fight, for Danny did not rise.

'Count!' Rivera cried hoarsely to the referee.

And when the count was finished Danny's seconds gathered him up and carried him to his corner.

'Who wins?' Rivera demanded.

Reluctantly the referee caught his gloved hand and held it aloft.

There were no congratulations for Rivera. He walked to his corner unattended, where his seconds had not yet placed his stool. He leaned backwards on the ropes and looked his hatred at them, swept it on and about him till the whole ten thousand gringos were included. His knees trembled under him, and he was sobbing from exhaustion. Before his eyes the hated faces swayed back and forth in the giddiness of nausea. Then he remembered they were the guns. The guns were his. The revolution could go on.

THE COMING RACE

E.G.E. BULWER-LYTTON

Tell me frankly what you saw in that chasm: I am sure it was something strange and terrible.' When the hero of this story, an American mining engineer, accompanies an acquaintance in the investigation of the dark recesses of the mine upon which his friend is employed, they come upon a vast subterranean kingdom, complete with roads, buildings, lakes, gigantic ferns and human-like creatures scuttling to and fro. Descending further by rope, his companion falls and plunges to his death. And then to his horror, the engineer sees a huge and terrible head, with open jaws and dull, ghastly, hungry eyes, emerging out of the darkness. He runs for safety, but when he returns not only has the body disappeared, but the rope has fallen and he no longer has any chance of return. He is alone in this strange world, in the bowels of the earth. . . .

First published in 1871, this pioneer work of science fiction describes a Utopian future civilization, based upon a renewable energy source Vril, and the conflict between this world and our own. Prescient for its time, this influential novel depicted a world of air travel and advanced technology and was also admired for its vivid recreation of sublime subterranean landscapes.

THE LOST WORLD and THE POISON BELT

ARTHUR CONAN DOYLE

The Lost World is the story of an expedition by four men to a remote plateau in South America, a region out of time, cut off from the outside world by unscaleable, vertical cliffs. In an area the size of an English county, pterodactyls, iguanodons, ape men and other dinosaurs still exist. Into this nightmare world come Professor Challenger, Summerbee, Lord John Roxton and the reporter Malone. After many adventures they return at last to London with proof of their incredible discovery.

On the anniversary of their first adventure, Professor Challenger draws together his fellow explorers, instructing them to bring oxygen. As reports come in of a world outbreak of illness, Professor Challenger surmises that the earth has swum into the poison belt: 'It is the end of the world' he pronounces. As the friends gather at Challenger's house, all around them appear to be dying. Will they too succumb?

Conan Doyle tried in vain to kill off his more famous creation, Sherlock Holmes, but in the character of Challenger he was content.

FROM EARTH TO MOON AND A TRIP ROUND IT

JULES VERNE

There is no one among you who has not seen the Moon . . . only enter into my plans and I will lead you to its conquest' proclaimed President Barbicane to fellow members of the Gun Club in Baltimore. So it was that in the year 186– the battle to send a rocket to the moon was announced. Rapidly taken up by the press nationwide, soon the whole world became excited by the noble and unprecedented enterprise. The astronomers at the Cambridge Observatory acted as advisers, a massive call for public subscription to raise finance was begun, and the construction of the Columbiad was investigated and experimented upon by Barbicane, and his arch-rival, Captain Nicholl, a specialist plate-maker. Will they be able to reconcile their differences enough to build the rocket? Then into the fray comes Frenchman Michel Ardan, determined to be the first passenger. Will they ever reach their destination?

In these two companion books, by the author of Around the World in Eighty Days and Journey to the Centre of the Earth, Jules Verne percipiently forecast the first journey to the moon: man's first actual flight to the moon took almost exactly the same length of time as this fictional voyage.